GABRIEL MOUREY

MONADA

TRANSLATED BY
SHAWN GARRETT

AND WITH AN INTRODUCTION BY
BRENDAN CONNELL

MONADA

GABRIEL MOUREY (1865-1943), was born in Marseille, the son of a druggist. In 1883 his first collection of poems, *Voix éparses . . .* , was published by the Librairie des bibliophiles, the lavish printing likely having been carried out at his own expense. Closely associated with the Decadent and Symbolist movements, he was involved with many of the imminent writers of the day, and was a close friend of Jean Lorrain. He translated the Edgar Poe's complete poetry into French, wrote extensively on art, most especially on the decorative arts, and numerous volumes of both poetry and fiction, one of the most striking of which is his collection of short stories, *Monada* (1894). His other works of fiction include *Les brisants* (1896), and *Cœurs en détresse* (1898).

SHAWN GARRETT is a freelance editor, critic and short fiction aficionado. He currently co-edits the horror fiction podcast *Pseudopod* and posts weekly columns with *Rue Morgue.* His translations include Robert Scheffer's *Prince Narcissus and Other Stories* (Snuggly Books, 2019).

BRENDAN CONNELL has published numerous works of fiction and translations. The former includes *Unpleasant Tales* (Eibonvale Press, 2013). His translations include Guido Gozzano's Alcina and Other Stories (Snuggly Books, 2019).

To my dear, departed sister Susan M. Garrett—who was more important to me than the world, and is the major reason I became the person I now am. A shining light of the self-publishing world, good friend and wise counsel, she is missed more than she would have ever realized. A day doesn't go by that I do not think of her and I'm sorry she didn't live to see these translations.

—The Translator

CONTENTS

INTRODUCTION

*M*ONADA, for all its obscurity, is one of the great short story collections of the Decadent Movement. It was first published in 1894, by Paul Ollendorf, most, if not all, of the contents having previously appeared in periodicals of the day. Despite the book having run to at least three editions, at the time of this writing, only two copies of the original French of *Monada* are known to exist, one in Bibliothèque nationale de France, and the second, from which this excellent translation by Shawn Garret was made, in the Museumsgesellschaft, in Zürich.

The author of the collection, Gabriel Mourey (1865-1943), was born in Marseille, the son of a druggist. In 1883 his first collection of poems, *Voix éparses . . .* , was published by the Librairie des bibliophiles, the lavish printing likely having been carried out at his own expense. The following year, together with his friend Raoul Russel, a minor poet of the day, he launched *Mireille, revue des poètes marseillais,* which ran to eight issues, each of which featured work by both Mourey and Russel. At some point during the subsequent years he moved to Paris, in order to pursue a literary career and, in 1888, his second collection of poetry, *Flammes mortes*, was released, followed in 1889 by a translation of the complete poems of Edgar Poe, for which Josephin Paladan provided an introduction.

At this period, he was already well involved with the symbolist movement in Paris and, as the dedications in the present volume will attest, he was friends with many of the imminent symbolist and decadent writers of the day, including Jean Lorrain, with whom he carried on a lively correspondence.

In 1890 he began his career as an art critic, a label for which, in fact, he became best known. He took an especial interest in decorative arts, and wrote extensively on English art and artists, including Burne-Jones, Aubrey Beardsley, and Dante Gabriel Rossetti—a fact which also offers some insight to the title story in *Monada*, in which the heroine seems to have been extracted directly from a painting by the latter.

The sixteen stories in *Monada* range widely in theme, but are almost all marked by a melancholy mood—of things lost, of things missed. The dreamy portraiture of the title story fades into childhood memories, symbolist fables, bizarre vignettes. "Lord Sorry," originally published in the supplement to *La Lanterne*, 7 Septembre 1893, and which, when reprinted in the collection, the author dedicated to Henri Bauër, the illegitimate son of Alexander Dumas, presents us with one of the more intriguing decadent heroes, supposedly painted by Whistler, who, it should be noted, did in fact paint more than one portrait of Comte de Montesquiou-Fézensac, the partial model for J.-K. Huysmans character Des Esseintes. "The Pale Couple," originally published in *Gil Blas*, 5 Mars 1893, on the other hand, fittingly dedicated to Octave Mirbeau in the version in the collection, can certainly be counted as one of the most striking *contes cruels*. And in the final piece, "Revenge of the Light," originally published in *Gil Blas*, 26 Janvier 1894, and which, when reprinted in the collection, the author dedicated to Gustave Guiches, author of the outrageous novella *The Modesty of Sodom*, we find ourselves confronted with a metaphysical tale altogether unique, a story which seems to blaze with occult significance.

After the publication of *Monada*, Mourey went on to publish numerous works—a translation of Okakura Kakuzō's *The Book of Tea* (translated from the English version), a number of plays, collections of poetry, and a great many collections of essays. And though he also went on to publish a further seven volumes of fiction, it is in *Monada*, his first offering in that regard, that the Decadent style is most manifest. The volume, long and undeservedly forgotten, is certainly worthy of a well-placed position in the Decadent canon.

—Brendan Connell

MONADA

MONADA

ON an afternoon of this last autumn I met a few intimates in a vast studio with iron-gray walls of stone. The yellow rays of that supreme season for sunsets poured across the splendor of that somber occasion. A tall, Empire-style Psyche, bathed in the light of copper sphinxes, stood in a corner near a blue damask door of the same time period—a gloomy surface of impassive clarity, vibrating alone amidst the dull reflection of the walls.

We patricians of weary pleasures and harmonious undulations, gentlemen and artists of haughty distinction, were still moved by the noble beauty of certain portraits of aristocratic and prestigious grace, done in black pencil, which the painter had just shown us. We drifted, in a half-dream state, into broken threads of dormant talk that arise upon immersing oneself in the contemplation of such complex works of art, when an unexpected and apparently insignificant event suddenly excited our curiosity: a drapery of green velvet, veiling an easel, detached itself and fell crashing to the floor in a dark mass.

In a frame of dark oak, under a surface of glass that magnified the sun in its current agonies of dusk, a strange apparition revealed itself, an apparition that perfectly corresponded to the pained autumnal flare of rays dying in the west. We all shuddered, as if someone had actually just entered the room, bearing a sign of some inevitable destiny.

The apparition of a young woman appeared, as if through a doorway unexpectedly cracked open, piercing the dark, austere nudity of the walls. From her silent gait, the simplicity of her black clothes, and all the vagueness and discreetness of her attitude, one felt that she was a ghost conjured up by the strange room itself, by its powerful aura of mystery. A fragile specter who lived an intense internal life, no doubt devoured by a too-powerful flame which burned inside her whole being. Or else, what incurable evil, what force of consumption, could stain her cheekbones with such a livid red?

She appeared, carrying on a serving tray some cups and a white porcelain coffee pot limned with gold. She came, a favorite servant or a docile mistress, emerging from the unknown corners of the house, with libations intended for some unknown host. And who and where are *they*? Absent from the table which she walked toward, barely divined under the funerary shadows of dusk . . .

Tall, yet still she seemed bowed under the weight of an irremediable destiny. So slender and graceful that one was reminded of those flowers which fade in the light of funeral tapers. Her cheeks were sad, an enigmatic suffering wrinkled and whitened her lips, and from under her half-lowered eyelids, attentive only to the fragility of her burden, filtered a look of mistrustful sweetness, a stubborn and resigned pain. Might she not have borne vengeance, a philter of love or death to be later poured into the opaque whiteness of the cups held in her lean, too-long hands? Oh, her hands! Her hands . . . hands of a sister of charity who applied dressings to sickened souls, hands of a faithful servant who closes the final stare of a dead master and casts the shade of the shroud over the rigid face, hands of a complacent mistress skilled at voluptuous caresses . . .

Like the forehead of German virgins, her brow was heavy with grave mysticism and pensive purity, while the severe chin spoke of a dry cruelty that does not pardon evil obstinacy and stubbornness in perversity. The easy and complicated abandon of her ringed hair made her appear formidable, dangerous even. Bleach blonde, ancestral blonde, the blonde hair of a child, all slipped from her forehead and down along her cheeks in serpentine curls, sinuous undulations. At her neck they twisted into caressing knots. A melancholic lassitude lingered in them, for there on her shoulders they were mute gold against the black of her dress, like living jewels. Her tresses, alone, spoke without pretension. Did they not overcome the painful poem of her missed life, her sacrifices, her devotions, her regrets, and perhaps her remorse or her unsatisfied ardor? Under her hair's embrace, the oval of her face was emaciated, narrow and stretched. It was a face of mourning, where the trace of a great, dead happiness had left its imprint of gloomy joy. And that pale mouth, those bloodless lips . . . to be so bleached and bloodless it is necessary to believe that other lips, perpetually absent lips, came from the dark to kiss them at night, to drink their red life, came from the other side of the world perhaps . . . or from the grave . . .

"Is this the portrait of a dead woman?" asked one of us. "It looks like her soul is floating around the frame . . ."

And someone murmured, "The Sphinx!"

Another said: "Certain heroines of d'Aurevilly and Villiers de l'Isle-Adam have resigned and haughty faces, a strange mourning of suppressed grief, a dull revolt against life."

Then, under our curious inquiries, the painter related this tale:

She was named Monada and was directed to me by a young woman whose portrait I had just finished, and who had once spoken about her as a model capable of interesting me. "A striking profile and curious hair," she had said, but so vaguely that I immediately formulated an excuse for not receiving her. Two or three months passed and I forgot the name, that mysterious name which should have been fixed in my memory because it corresponded so well to my state of mind, to my intellectual concerns of that time . . .

At that time, you see, I had gone back to reading Poe. That miraculous work, which had so fascinated my adolescence, took up my whole life again. I spent my days in his intoxicating hallucinations, in the familiar anguish of those intimate nightmares where perhaps the greatest of modern geniuses poured out his frantic soul. Very often I had said to myself:

"In the presence of Ligeia, Beatrix, Morella or Eleonora, what magic brush would a painter require if called upon to fix their supernatural features? The sickly charm of their grace, the gloomy glow of their smile, ah! How sweet it would be to be able to contemplate them, to be able to be perpetually intoxicated by their image . . . even unto death!"

That thought had become an obsession and one evening, an evening on an autumn Sunday suffused with the same rusty light as this one, I was rereading those sentences which I now know by heart:

> *A singular* intensity *in the thought, in the action, in the speech, had perhaps in it the result or at least the index of this gigantic power of volition which, during our long relations, could have given other and more positive proofs of its existence. Of all the women I knew, she, the always placid Ligeia, on the outside so calm, was the prey most torn by the tumultuous vultures of the cruel passion. And I could only evaluate this passion by the miraculous expansion of her eyes that delighted and frightened me at the same time, by the almost magical melody, the modulation, the sharpness and the placidity of her deep voice— and by the wild energy of strange words that she usually pronounced and whose effect was doubled by the contrast of her flow.*

Yes, that evening, as I reread those evocative sentences, a familiar haunting that had infernally tortured me, resumed.

All of a sudden, there was a ring at my door. For a moment I hesitated to get up but . . . what was happening? An invisible hand took mine, made me go through the studio, led me to the door and forced me to open it wide, while usually I only unseal it a crack. In the doorway, amidst the smothering shadow of the staircase, a woman stood motionless, an indecisive smile on her lips, dark in her black clothes of religious austerity. "Ligeia! Ligeia!" murmured a similarly dark voice in my ear. "Ligeia! As you were dreamed in the magical phrases of the story-teller," and joy flooded my soul.

She took a step forward, entered my home in silence, and not a word came from me . . . I was dumbstruck with happiness.

However, she sat . . . there . . . in that armchair, or rather no, on the *edge* of that armchair, because I have never seen her sit on a seat where she didn't give the impression of barely leaning, just as she always seemed to walk on tiptoe, a few inches from the ground, as if a ghost. As soon as she reclined, she named herself to me.

"Yes, Monada," I stammered, "I remember . . . I recognize you."

She did not show any surprise. With a great calm, and without stopping for a moment to look me in the eyes with that gaze that seemed to search one's soul even to its darkest corners, she asked me . . . if it might not please me if she posed . . . her friend Madame de X had told her that she'd spoken to me about it . . . She would consider herself quite happy if I agreed to it . . . Her voice echoed like voices we hear in dreams, and I dared not answer. What answer could there be? I only bowed in response.

"It shall be so, then!" she continued. "Here I am, entirely at your pleasure. When do we work?"

"Tomorrow, if you'd like."

She repeated my words: "Tomorrow, yes, I will enjoy that. Ah, I forgot . . . there is the question of remuneration . . . we will not talk about it, if you do not mind . . . it does not interest me . . . no, no, do not try to insist. Besides, there are too many vain words spoken."

She paused, looked around her for a long time, hardly turning her head, as if she had been endowed with a visual sense more acute than an ordinary human eye . . . because she questioned me immediately about a canvas placed almost behind her, which I had sent to the Salon the previous year. Then, stilling herself again, her black-gloved fingers began to caress the blonde serpents of her hair, and for the first time a shy look crept into the edge of her mouth as she said:

"Oh! I have to tell you . . . I'm very curious." She lowered her beautiful eyelids (and it was like a shadow suddenly descending across her face), "Yes, very curious . . . I would like to know if there is between us a thoughtful and passionate understanding of the arts . . . ? As for me . . ."

And in a few words she revealed a prodigious understanding, an exaltation more intuitive than I have ever heard from any woman, without any snobbery and with accents of ardent sincerity at which she blushed somewhat. None of the customary trivialities of her sex seemed to occupy her, there was no coquetry, and yet she knew how to remain a woman of exquisite femininity, rare and incomprehensible. Those were overwhelming, superhuman minutes, and I grieved to listen to her, sometimes contenting myself with directing her thought to some other aesthetic realm, at which she again exalted, seized with a sort of vertigo, all transfigured.

There are, in the field of art, certain summits which remain forbidden to a whole race of minds. Such individuals, even superior ones, cannot attain it. The atmosphere one breathes in would suffocate them. I speak specifically of those *confessional* works, if I may call them that, which contain a sacramental mystery. Works like certain passages of Bach, Beethoven, Schumann and Wagner in music, like the *San Giovanni* of Leonardo da Vinci, for example, in painting, and in literature the second *Faust*, *The Temptation of St. Anthony*, *Axël* or *The Master Builder*. Well, just like initiates read the spirit of eternal mysteries in the structures of ancient temples, so Monada had managed to free from these masterpieces the blinding splendor of the symbols they conceal. She had known how to penetrate their religious sense, their metaphysical enigmas.

"Do you not think," she asked with emotional simplicity, "that we learn much more about the mystery of life and death in four or five of Beethoven's last quartets, or in those two, so poignant pages of the book where Tristan awakens, wounded, on the terrace where the song of the shepherd still rings, or in the defeated, illuminated and ecstatic smile of *Beata Beatrix* by Rossetti, than in the depth of the divinatory philosophies?"

As she spoke, I enjoyed contemplating her. She differed strangely from this portrait here: her eyes were full of sincere flames, and there was in her every gesture, in her manner of frequently inclining her body to the left as if the burden of her heart at that moment tired her, in the whole of her person, a kind of special harmony, of rhythmic suppleness which I found myself powerless to translate to the canvas, here. The soft intonations of her voice sometimes became suddenly wild and hoarse and, at the end of her sentences, there were occasional drops of agony, a failing darkness, and she would then close her eyes as if faced with some clarity which blinded her.

She returned the next day, and I waited for her feverishly. She came, but she was so different from what she had been the day before. On entering, she said:

"I must beg your pardon for my exuberance yesterday. It must have seemed ridiculous to you, from an unknown woman . . . excuse me, will you?"

And she enthusiastically shook my hand.

The painter broke off. A faint smile floated on his lips and then, a little moved, he resumed:

Ah, that ineffable moment of divine anguish when one finds oneself for the first time before the model, brush in hand! A kind of delicious terror invades you. Between the painter and the model there is an exchange of etheric fluid, of spiritual penetration which, in an intuitive artist, signifies a great deal for the eventual success of the work he is about to undertake. Powerful minutes where all our strength of cerebration is focused by our gaze on the thrilling human form there, until the synthesis consistent with the dream of realization that we ourselves imposed becomes suddenly clear. In front of Monada, that day, I felt the strangest sensations, something painful and exultant. Anguish oppressed my heart while my head, happily, blazed. Never before had both the pitiful weakness and the haughty grandeur of the artist, present before the life he wanted to tame, manifested itself to me.

Alas, my delirium was short-lived! A terrible struggle had just begun between Monada and myself, a struggle which was to last three whole weeks and from which I emerged triumphant, but only after much suffering! I told you, did I not, the change that had taken place in Monada's whole person between her first and second visit? Literally, she was not the same anymore. Of all the characteristics of her gesture, her attitude, the particular harmony of her whole being which had so much exalted me on the first day, there was no longer any vestige. I made superhuman efforts to bring a smile to her lips, to capture with the brush that look, from the immobile opal of her eyes, the complex charms of which had obsessed me. But all in vain. She appeared to me as if sealed behind a cold oath, sheltering herself under the rigidity of an impassive mask on which nothing remained—alive, animated—of all that made her who she was. The half-tones of thought, the sudden ardor of sensations, all the infinite and perpetual ebb of a soul guised in a human being, really seemed to have withered in her. Twenty times I resumed the same preparatory studies without being able to rediscover the image of that first day. Monada was no longer there in front of me. Another woman emanated from her, one she scarcely resembled, an inaccurate and troubled reflection of the Monada of yore, indifferent and almost banal. She stubbornly refused to manifest, suspicious and cruel, a voluntary frown on her forehead.

Finally, exasperated one day, I threw my palette and brushes into a corner of the studio and started to cry with rage.

She came to me, softly, and rested her hand on my shoulder.

"Why are you suffering?" she asked, her voice caressing, sincere and deep as that first day. "Tell me, what are you suffering from?"

Then, brutally, I lost control of myself and accused her. I violently and outrageously reproached her for the torment which she had inflicted on me for three weeks, her perpetual flight to escape from my scrutiny . . . the miserable abortion of work that I could realize so easily if she wanted me to.

I must have found words of unmistakable sincerity, for she seemed to faint. She put her hand to her heart in a desperate, crushed gesture and moved away from me, prey to a mute and cold pain that, eventually, returned her likeness to that of the initial evening when she had appeared. But was I, myself, sincere in my anger? To this day I still wonder, and everything that has happened forces me to answer that, No, I was not sincere. A ruse, that suffering that made me sob. A cheat, that discouragement which inspired me to such a tragic gesture. How could I not see it then? How could I not, on seeing her defeated thus, throbbing with pity and emotion for me, how could I not all at once have understood (if there had been even the slightest truth in my despair) the abyss of love from which she held out her supplicating arms to me? For a few moments she remained there, a few yards from me, beautiful with happy pain, her hands full of consolation and tenderness, and it would have been enough just for me to come to her, drink the salt of her tears, place my pleading forehead against her wet cheek, lower her fevered hair . . . and Monada would have belonged to me . . . maybe . . . ! Ah, those looks in which I could read so much love had become precious to me! But can we learn the science of guessing the secrets of souls? This gesture to dare, this word to utter, this circumstantial game in which so many other men show such irresistible skill, would I ever have been able to accomplish it, had the opportunity manifested itself to me?

Alas, she almost immediately resumed her indifferent attitude! Again, following this fugitive abandonment whose meaning escaped me, the mask of icy coldness and impassivity drew over her face. Once again, she was the cruel and murderous Monada, with a cold profile and a closed soul.

From that day on our relations established a kind of dull rancor, a regret for a scene that had left behind a bitterness we shared between us. Especially on Monada's side. I noticed the strange way that she always seemed to try and thwart me, at everything and nothing. It was like she had become an enemy to me. And yet, on the other hand, when she posed she had begun to yield a little. Day by day, that Monada of old returned imperceptibly, until the day when I finally possessed her, complete, in the abandonment to her mysterious, complex beauty, that was both a little funereal and fatal. But as I saw her giving herself up, surrendering herself to me, I noticed on her face and in her self the traces of an acute and incomprehensible suffering. A fever encircled her eyelids with a halo of mourning, her eyes clouded with haunting tears, and her movements were weighted with a discouraged lassitude, an insurmountable weakness that broke the general harmony of her form. Never had she appeared to me so exasperatingly beautiful.

Then, for the first time, I became curious to know all that I did not know about her, her way of life, her past, the secrets of the existence of her whose strangeness almost worried me. How and on what did she live? What could her material resources be? What atrocious customs of debauchery and vice hid in her enigmatic appearance? And, in truth, I enjoyed degrading her in my dissolute suppositions. Assuredly, there must have been in her life some abject, unspeakable affair, the remorse from which had thusly exhausted her. Ah, what infamy would I not allow myself to suspect of her when she arrived weary, as if she were blissful with voluptuousness? Just as it had been precious to judge her superior to all, to halo her forehead with an immaculate light, so I now lowered myself to consider her only as a creature worthy of all pity and contempt. "Bah!" I said to myself, "after all, what does her story matter? She offers, when I really look at it, enough exterior charm for the work I want to accomplish. What more should I wish for?" The grudge I held against her, for the torture she had imposed on me for so many days, now prevented me from being otherwise interested in her, except for what was needed in the completion of the portrait.

Our relations remained extremely cold. She arrived exactly at the appointed hour, immediately took the pose, which she held with scrupulous rigor, and only left at nightfall. A handshake on arrival and departure, a few indifferent words exchanged through closed lips, that was where our intimacy was now confined.

One day she came later than usual. She dragged her steps more slowly, more nonchalantly. It seemed as if an overwhelming burden weighed on her, inexorably weakened her. I cannot help but remember the slightest details of this interview, which was our last. I can still see her face: her eyes burnt out, her nose pinched by insomnia, prey to one of those fits that put a maddening seduction of secret pain in women's faces. Only, on that one day, had I the consciousness that there was something else in her life, outside of the weaknesses and shame I had so unfairly accused her of, but what? A drama perhaps, but what tragedy was she struggling with, if she even had the strength to continue to struggle, for she seemed to me exhausted, broken, lost, desperate.

As soon as she entered, she was immediately more affectionate than usual. She came to stand in front of the portrait and contemplated it for a long time, which she had not done for a fortnight at least. Then, in an almost playful voice, which contrasted strangely with the dismal distress spread by her whole being, she said:

"Well, are you happy, my friend? Satisfied with me . . . and yourself? . . . When do you hope to finish? Tomorrow, the day after tomorrow? Please do not be angry; I assure you I am merely impatient and it is not because of you that I ask, just that I feel mortally tired . . . of what? Do not ask. But you will never know the price of the sacrifice I have been making for two months . . . and then, would you even understand if I were weak enough to reveal it to you?"

At these words, she burst into tears and threw herself into an armchair, her head in her hands, shaking and panting with spasms. For a long time she cried from her very depths, in a most moving display of feminine pain. Her serpentine ringlets bit her, struck at her, embraced her with their caresses and fled from her face as if their bites had increased her torture. I remained standing, silent, looking at her, not daring to speak or move and powerless to find a consoling word or gesture, as one stands before a suffering, twisting patient when one is unaware of the ailment or the remedy. Alas, do you know anything more cruel than to witness a pain that we don't understand?

Little by little, however, she calmed down. I smiled as her eyes awakened under the dying storm of her tears. At last, with a violent effort and an agonized voice, one of those voices that remain unforgettable because we feel that they sound the death knell of a lifetime, she said:

"I ask you a thousand times for forgiveness . . . a thousand times for forgiveness . . . my friend. But there are days when there is something more powerful in me than myself, and it begins to take me over, to own me . . . haven't you noticed it already? And I do give in, despite myself. I must have hurt you a great deal . . . but if you knew how much I did to myself . . . So . . . I would desire that you hold no grudge . . . I'm sorry . . ."

She was silent. Then, when it seemed that she had forcibly decided all that she must or must not confess, she continued:

"When I see myself like this, as a little girl . . . but it would be too long to tell you . . . At an age when we are all still soft wax under the brutal fingers of reality, already I was taken by uprisings against life. I tried to dominate myself, in vain . . . do you not find that we always remain, despite our education and years, as we once were, that is to say a child? Certainly, at that time one has all one's future . . . or rather, no, one *contains* all one's future. For me, it must have been written that I must suffer from everything, that my destiny is to be unhappy. So much so, in fact, that any good one seeks to do for me, destiny necessarily changes it into evil . . . yes, it is written that I must suffer from everything, everything in the world, even happiness . . ."

In finishing these words she blanched with suppressed rage. Her mouth opened and closed in agony and she dropped her arms rigidly at her sides in a frightful fit of immobility. She remained silent for a long time, and yet I still seemed to hear her soul's complaint, that melody of sorrow that escaped from her lips just as the blood flows from a fresh wound.

"Monada," I called in a low voice, "will you allow me to suffer from your pain?"

And I knelt before her. I wanted to take her hand, but she immediately pushed me aside with a brief gesture.

"Monada," I repeated, "yes, I finally understand you, I've figured it out, but too late . . ."

And again, I do not know what boldness pushed me, I put my hand on hers. Then a shudder ran through her, and she got up suddenly, her face convulsed, terrible.

"Leave me, leave me," she said, wringing her arms, "leave me," and she ran her fingers over her eyes as if to chase away a cursed vision. "Leave me! Do not utter a single word. I will see you tomorrow."

She headed for the door. For a moment I was about to join her, to take her in my arms and force her to stay. But, no, I watched her leave, without daring anything. She did not even turn back before she disappeared.

"I will see you tomorrow," she said.

Ah, the agonizing hours I lived during the day that followed. I could not remember when the thought of a woman had ever imposed such atrocious ideas on me. Sometimes I felt my whole self crumbling at the whim of this enigmatic creature, thirsty for my suffering while wearing a smile of triumph on her lips, that sweet, grave, deep smile that I knew. But then, I also became incapable of regaining composure. I envisioned myself trampled under her feet, a palpitating, shapeless wreck, like the nameless flesh that butchers throw to the dogs. Sometimes, by a sudden and formidable concentration of my will into an impulse of avenging hatred, she was mine to roughly caress, to strangle with embraces, to devour in bites. What an unearthly, infinite voluptuousness I felt as the tamed body of the young woman struggled against me. And, suddenly, her resistance would blossom into the most tender consent. She knotted her arms around my neck and whispered confident inflections with all the ardor of her wild nature in her strange voice, the mystery torn from her heart. Whispers in which I heard the history of a most sumptuous life, the most complex poetry of soul a human being could be part of. The secret of her prodigious brain, her exceptional faculty of understanding that enabled her to raise her fragile female being from mere woman to a metaphysical ecstasy in which she communed on the summits with the flaming souls of the most powerful djinns. That secret she finally revealed to me, by speaking of her dramatic pain, for isn't it only by pain that human education is enlarged and completed unto the definitive possession of the divine world?

Alas, the next day Monada did not reappear, nor the day after, nor again, and I experienced the torture of the acutest regrets. I had let a miraculous creature pass me by without possessing anything of her, as if I had stood at the door of a closed palace whose internal splendors one can only guess at, and never knocked. A fading sense of superhuman clarity, an obsession with a gloomily radiant memory, that's all of her that remained for me.

I spent fifteen days of melancholy spleen and discouragement. I spent those days calling out to her, begging aloud to her. The hope of a letter from her sometimes drew me from this painful sluggishness, and I envisioned future projects. I saw her return, sitting in her usual place, so deeply attractive and disturbing . . . and we resumed our familiar dialogues from the first days. I made myself the gentlest and most reserved of men, so as not to frighten her delicate expansiveness. Then I began to desire her, to love her, and I concentrated all my powers of affection, of devotion, of submissive tenderness on her. I remained for hours at a time contemplating the portrait, which had become all the more dear to me as it reminded me of her and all the suffering I was now grateful that she had inflicted on me. "Monada! Monada!" I said in a low voice, "what harm have I caused you to justify such reprisals? No, I do not misunderstand you, you must know that. Your tears, fallen on my heart, have so generously seeded it! From my selfishness, my hardships, you made the refreshing source of pity spring forth, and I have learned from you to cherish Pain. Along with you, I rose far away from common men, in contempt of all that remains vain, useless and foreign to the enrichment of a creature of the elite. You have taught me the legitimate pride that one feels in becoming aware of oneself, knowing how to judge oneself and judging others. O Monada, you have saved me from myself, by reviving my faculty of enthusiasm which was so long dried up. I listened too much to men, with their frivolous words, their vulgar effusions. I sought their esteem and suffered from their disdain. Thanks to you, I have become the creature of abundant and sovereign sensibility that one *must* be to approach God. And I bless you, and I love you. The purest and most ardent memory of you will remain in me. Forgive me for the foolish desires I once defiled you with, and now, forever, be the thricefold glorious Sister to whom I owe this life in the hereafter, beyond dream and love."

Thus, I addressed the image of Monada. Kneeling before it, it seemed that the picture had become animated and the frail young woman stepped down to me, spoke softly to me with such words! Words which I must keep secret! From her divine hands she poured the balm of consolation and hope. I became accustomed, gradually, to living with her dear ghost. My exaltations melted into a voluptuous tranquility, into a spiritual, permanent and moving joy. With these delicate chiaroscuro sensations, my whole being recovering after supreme crises . . . I lived like that for two months, or a full ninety days after Monada's departure.

And at last, one day—having spent a night of insomnia, a night of agitation and vague presentiment like those that precede the irrational expectation of some great happiness or irreparable misfortune—one day I received a letter from her, dated from Liverpool. I will read it to you. Here it is:

And the painter, having risen, drew Monada's letter from the drawer of a bureau. Then, very pale, standing near the large bay window where the night had almost fallen, his hands trembling as they clutched the pages that awoke so much pain and regret, he read in a hesitant voice:

"My friend, many days ago, exactly three months since our last interview, I find I am fighting against myself in writing to you. It was necessary that time flowed over our common wounds, so that I might happily do now what I had sworn I would not do. Between beings of our moral worth, incapable of disloyalty, whose lofty view causes us to despise nearly everything about life, there are special duties which no one but ourselves have the right to enact. That is why it feels so sweet, and it seems to me now so noble, to fail at my own oath. Not by cowardice, please believe me, because all suffering remains for me—especially that which you caused yourself!—in trying to relieve my suffering with a confession—and such a confession!—but because the irresistible logic of my destiny demands that I now accomplish the exact opposite of what you yourself might judge fit to accomplish.

"Friend, would it bring you great, great happiness (and could you enjoy, like me, this happiness if it was real but unobtainable?) if you learned that there was a woman in the world for whom you had become the only thought and only love, the thought and love of all of her life now . . . and that this woman's name is Monada? Ah, please wait, my lips burn with these words, and I am quite startled by my heartbeat!

"Yes, I love you. Now you understand that I had to betray my promise in order to, first, save myself from remorse—do I have the right to refuse you this joy, if you can experience it—in knowing that Monada loves you deliriously! Secondly, and above all, because it would become impossible for me to live with the obsession of this suffocating thought, from too much sweetness, knowing that I love you, that I love you.

"Yes, I love you, in the deepest and most superhuman sense of this word so often blasphemed. Yes, I love you, I repeat it with courage, since we must never see each other again. I cry this word to you through the immensity which separates us, from all the force of my being, and—alas!—for the first and last time. I dream of you reading these lines, so far from me, there in your studio where the best of what I can be lives again, with a bit of my suffering and tears, and I wonder, with anguish: 'After the adored tortures of our daily interviews, after the hell of these three months far from each other, would a curse give rise to a smile of pity on his lips at this confession, in case he himself would not be, like me, driven by a delirium to proclaim the same divine words, in case he would not love me as much as I love him? . . . Ah, if you possessed the cruelty! . . . This idea alone freezes my soul. I remember, one day, you read a letter in feminine writing while in my presence, while satisfied pride flamed on your face . . . Oh, how I hated you, despised you, for the unconscious admission of inferiority that escaped you! I loved you too much, even then, not to remember this now and weep. So, my friend, tell me if the same thoughts come back to you now, that I saw assault you then? Oh, I beg you, I beg you on my knees to tear this up without reading any further! I feel, despite our distance, the pain of humiliation. Spare me, if you can, unless . . . but why fear such tortures from you? Because I have allowed you to think, on my behalf, of far too many unfavorable things and the coming of this letter with its follies allow you to believe even more. Since none of your thoughts escaped me, I witnessed your suffering and your hatred and I keep the certainty that you suffered and hated as much as possible, suffered from me or rather because of me, hated the fierce and bloody resistance with which I opposed you. Men always hold it against women to not perpetually appear the same as they dream they are, or as they saw them the first time. For you, there are other reasons that justify: your obsession with an artistic dream that you hoped to create, thanks to me, and my stubbornness in holding back. Happily, it seems to me that you did not guess my real motive. It was because I began to love you in an intolerable way. I was afraid of myself, and my only defense was to impose on you a different image of Monada, because the constant effort of my will to do so forbade all dangerous exaltation.

"Tell me, my friend, in these weeks have you realized the harshness of this internal struggle? I knew I was defeated before I started, but I was thirsty for heroism. Alone, away from your company, I suffered the frightful torment of weakness, exhaustion, incapable of resuming the grueling battle from one day to the next. But as soon as I had crossed the threshold of your house, as soon as I put my foot on the first step of your staircase, oh, what a wind of courage carried me away! I was anxious to find myself in front of you, as one desires to see a mortal enemy, in order to better savor one's vengeance. But, unfortunately, how vain this all was, on the day I got the opportunity to measure your suffering, the suffering you thought I was happy to cause you. Presented with your tears, what could I do? Resist? My own tears informed you of my defeat. Never had such anguish strangled a human being. I looked at you, as we look at the fire that is going to devour us. For a moment, although you had not moved, I felt your two arms around my neck, felt the joy of being crushed by caresses, your caresses, the delirium of melting under your embrace. But you spared me that, and I loved you more from that day, as I finally became enlightened to myself. While giving all myself up to you, and while never ceasing to love you, I regained my courage. I was no longer afraid of myself, I was only afraid of you. A great assurance strengthened me, the assurance that one can always find the strength to resist others, even you, more victoriously than oneself.

"And now, my friend, there is a question that I see rising to your lips and which I must answer, so that you can keep your esteem of me whole and not think what this letter authorizes you to think of me as you might think of another.

"'Monada, tell me,' you say, 'why did you leave? Why, loving me with the irresistible love you confess, why did you not consent to stay with me? Life would have been sweet for both of us, and you would have belonged to me, body and soul?' That's the question I give you the right to ask of me. Well, notwithstanding all the folly of loving you, in spite of this delirium which overwhelms me in remembering you, dreaming of the deepest intoxication which I know you might never have satisfied in me, no, it could never have occurred. Monada would never have belonged to you. Not, my dear beloved, that there could exist in this world another man in whose arms it would be divine to feel myself dying, but because every possession of one being by another, even to an equal degree of intellectual or moral superiority, all possession debases and diminishes. The carnal slavery in which women indulge men seems to me the most irremediable shame. They are possessed but never possess. Unconscious, incapable of any return to themselves or of any impartial examination of what they have become, once one is a mistress of a man (the words have strange ironies) they are enslaved, subjected, reduced to the lower role of an instrument of pleasure. I know that they throw a veil of illusion on themselves with words that they believe to be sincere, that they try to hide their humiliation, and that they almost always succeed, until they are proud of their master. Would you have liked this from Monada? Although I love you beyond all imagination, the thought alone that a moment would come when you would have had the right to demand it almost makes me hate you. Possessed by you, I was immediately worth less than you. I suddenly became your inferior, while my joy and pride were that you judged me your equal.

"As a little girl, I witnessed my mother's perpetual slavery under my father's carnal domination. My passionate life later recalled this example. With my precocious child's eyes, I could sense the meaning of imploring glances, gestures of desire, words in a low voice, with which she begged my father . . . and those shudders that ran through her all the time when he came home and leaned down to kiss her, the sudden pallor which transfigured her, made her a creature no longer of herself but living only for the will of another being, her trainer. Later, I remembered all that. As I learned more about life, the mysterious sense of my impressions of those days was illuminated and I was ashamed of my mother, shamed and pitiful! God knows how much worship I had devoted to her, to that sweet and tender woman! As for my father, in spite of his profound kindness to me, I was never anything but an enemy. I judged him incapable of all nobility, of all elevation of spirit, of any moral value, and saw him ceaselessly imposing the humiliation and debasement of his attentions on a woman whom he professed to love. It was then that I swore to myself a promise which no man in the world, not even you my beloved friend, would be strong enough to make me violate.

"Alone in the world, absolute mistress of my actions, with enough fortune to possess the widest independence, nothing would have the power to stop any impulse of my desires. What women call their duty, or their honor, does not exist for me. I do not recognize as superior laws before which I must bow, only those which I dictate to myself.

"I have guarded my soul from you for such a long time that you could hardly have guessed at my true self. It has pleased me to confess to you, today, in loyal and complete sincerity, the further proof of my love for you! I know the suffering that the future holds for me, I know the torment of my future hours subsuming this passion for you that burns in my entire being.

"But, did I not tell you once, and can you now ignore, that fate requires me to suffer from everything in the world, even and above all happiness? . . . You, my soul, please be happy. And if life becomes cruel to you, if misfortune assails you, then remember Monada. But, she asks from her knees, think of her only in suffering. She loves you too much to want to share anything other than your tears, and you would not be so ungracious as to take away her part.

"Farewell, my beloved friend. Tomorrow I shall have left Europe, and we will not see each other again. Look at me sometimes, in the portrait where you have forever fixed me, and think that nothing in the world will break a bond like ours. We cried together. As I dwell on the canvas—your work!—I want to be forever for you something like an inaccessible queen, who comes with joy to serve you in the pose that I chose, as a spiritual servant, in all the ardor of my love. Farewell!

"Monada.

"Thus ended the story of Monada," the painter said, folding the letter as he tried to smile, but tears trembled in his eyes.

Night had come down. Scarcely a reflection of day was left scattered in the vast studio, quickly devoured by the austerity of the iron-gray walls. A uniform gloom from the angles of the room came towards us, gradually tightening like the devouring shadow of a mouth. One could hardly distinguish the fading profile of a face, the gesture of a hand limned with gloomy light, the intermittent flash of a cigarette, and we were all silent. An assembly of ghosts moved by the silence, and only one being really seemed to live there, the enigmatic young woman, the haughty and strange Monada who stood in the shadows, in the triumph of her sickly beauty . . . and that invocation came out of one of our mouths:

"*Holy Monada, pray for us.*"

THE SEDUCTION OF REFLECTIONS

For J.-H Rosny

THIS is a story of my childhood, full of naïve sweetness and poignant simplicity.

Two little girls and I were in a clearing at sunset, not far from the family home. Sitting, all three, in front of the wisteria wall that separated the park from the road, we watched the calm landscape gradually fade away. At the end of the plain, low hills outlined their sharp peaks on the golden background of the sky, and the sun, through a bouquet of pines above us, seemed an enormous fruit of light.

A silent gravity weighed between us, something like the sadness that comes over the livestock in the evening. They, eleven and twelve, myself scarcely fourteen, did we already feel, despite our ignorance, the painful weight of life? Instinctive fears, no doubt, a fatal anxiety of scattered mysteries . . . or what? . . . A profound foreknowledge of the coming tears that too soon furrow the brows of the young . . . ?

Of my two friends, Renée and Thérèse, the latter evoked tenderness in me.

With her long black hair like a flag of darkness, her overly-rosy complexion, her overly-joyous eyes, her perpetual laughter, and all her exuberance, Renée frightened me. I could tell that her blood was too ardent, as she was always eager for movement and insatiable for games.

Contrarily, Thérèse's sickly grace attracted me irresistibly, her slightest gesture marked by melancholic nobility. She walked slowly, wearily, spoke little and in a disappointed voice, and only cherished things for their weakness or gentleness. She seemed to live in a pale dream. All violence hurt her fragile being; she would have fainted at a sudden cry and the harsh glare of the summer sun caused her dangerous troubles. She loved to spend her days in the dim, shuttered light of a vast, cool Louis XVI salon, with its light wood paneling, ribboned cretonne panels, and rustic attributes. A profusion of mirrors multiplied the vision indefinitely, and their sleepy shimmer delighted the little girl. At the end of the day, it was her joy to contemplate the reflection of the landscape framed by the open windows: the high trees of the park, the statues and the stone vases, the slenderness of the fountains' jets of water, the pure line of the hills. She remained motionless for long hours, carried away in the vertigo of reflections: reflections of the sky and herself, reflections of furniture and herself, reflections from all around her

. . . and of herself . . . Then a smile illuminated her face, through happy tears.

Poor little child of melancholy, how often did the desire come to me, in crepuscular hours, to nestle my head against your heart!

Unconsciously, by the example of your ecstasies, you taught me life. Did not your contemplative silences fully signify that it is only in the mirror of our thoughts and of our hearts that it is useful and beautiful to look at the world?

As the ripe fruit of the sun had just fallen behind the horizon, we all rose up. Renée was running ahead, Thérèse and I were walking side by side, indolently.

Before we reached the green shade of the park, she wanted to look one last time at the twilight sky. Clouds ran, pink, among the liquid gold: it looked like a fairy sea that furrows under the flight of large ships. Very slowly, barely balanced in their rhythm, they crossed an immense gulf to take refuge behind the high cliffs of gray clouds that their passage had fringed with sparkling foam.

Ah! Dear little one, in the depths of miseries and passions you always appear to me as you did that evening, which was to be your last. In your deep, sweet voice I hear you say the fatal words to me: "Oh, let's go see the boats from the sky swim in the pond!" And it was suddenly like a madness in you, you leaning at the edge of the water to follow them. Renée joined us in a frolic: "How stupid you are, Thérèse, how stupid!" she said, seeing you squatting on the shore, plunging your eager glance into the burning abyss. What delusions transfigured you! An unknown light shone in your face, beneath the large mound of hair with flowers in it which sheltered your vague features in shadows. In your long dress of light cloth with small bouquets, your frail body seemed like that of a bird trying its wings, and your ribbons floated in the breezes of the falling night. And the mirage tempted you.

In the liquid mirror, a magnificent ship was sailing at full speed, with blazing banners of fire.

"What are you stupid, Thérèse? Oh, how stupid you are!" Renée kept repeating, and I remember that I pinched her arm to silence her, so beautiful did you look in your childishness. Ah! If I had known how to understand you then, if I had known how to share your joy, cry as you did, or even if I could recover your tears, instead of letting them lose themselves in the eternal infinity of the water! . . . If I had known! Did not your tears of that moment, your supreme tears, contain the balm for my future wounds, the cordial for the despair that awaited me? For my unhealthy drought, they would be today the fertilizing dew, and I would grow strong in the Ideal! But no . . .

The dinner bell rang suddenly. Renée was already far away. We were both alone, bending over the divine abyss of heaven. And the bell rang, like a knell. The great ship left behind, among the liquid gold of the sea, only a brilliant wake. One step more. You leaned forward, arms extended, and the weight of your dream dragged you away. The mystery of the water closed. I remained there a few moments, inert, my feet like lead. Then I suddenly ran off towards the family home, shouting of the misfortune. Alas! It was too late.

But your memory flourishes in me, little child of melancholy, better than the lessons of dry philosophers. Now that years have passed, nothing funerary or even painful is left to me of you. And how could I regret you? Have you not left intact in me the beautiful treasure of your own ardor that life would have squandered? Your soul survives still in the memory of my heart.

THE BLACK CHILD

For Paul Adam

THAT night the King did not sleep.

Three times he had the lamps, which were at-tached to the beams of cedar that were inlaid with gold, re-lit. Three times he had them extinguished. A fever burned in his blood, made his breath crackle, his temples ache: it seemed to him that the royal headdress that had just left him was still present in the flesh, made of red iron. And in his empty—or perhaps too full—head he thought he heard a murmur, perhaps the silken flight of some memory. But this murmur grew, became the sound of a river overflowing the plains; and he rose, opening the stained-glass window to see: at the bottom of the walls the river glided calmly, but that noise became tremen-dous, the rolling carts of an army on the march, the con-fused but enormous clamor of a besieged city, battering rams shaking the ramparts, chunks of rock bursting the domes, and he thought he saw the heavy Jewish columns that supported the hall crumble away. He remembered Samson. Why? There was no Delilah for him.

And he had the nightlights lit again. Lying more peacefully on a heap of cushions suspended in a hammock, with leather thongs adorned in purple, to pillars of gilded iron, he dreamt.

He was dreaming. Filtered lunar rays drew on the floors strewn with precious powders, the colorful fantasy of the stained glass. And his dream, his dream of Martyrdom of the Throne, the great slave of the glittering Past and the ancestral Glory, his dream of a Man-God in front of whom pale herds of kings, his dream enslaved itself to the small plates of light where the moon shone on the precious powders of the parquet floors.

Remembrance of his youth assailed him, drowned in a haze of years: he remembered free walks; wandering in the open countryside; cool stops under the saluting palms of the oases. Nights slept on the breast of a little slave whom he had met one evening, and who immediately loved him with all her gazelle soul. She had deep, clear dark eyes, huge eyebrows, a blood red mouth, a tawny mane that made her a sister of the lovely lionesses.

Here the woof of memories was broken; a wide rift through which his anxious memory passed and passed in vain: the song she sang, her song, the wild and luminous song with which she cradled him in her arms in the evenings, seated on the threshold in front of the dry road where the caravans go. The song of sun and love that he stopped with a kiss on her lips, a warm kiss, all singing in his voice. The song, the song; at times he felt it beat in his ears. He thought he was seizing it, the fleeting chant of old times that had enamored his heart.

She, she must have died.

This memory was expelled. The majesty of the King was troubled and he sent for the Rhapsod. He was a young stranger of high birth, with a magical voice and the heart of a poet, who was always wounded and whose soul had known how to please the King's.

He came and sang accompanied by a mandore.

> *Said the Black Child: Love me, love me!*
> *My heart is a wonderful black dahlia*
> *which only once must bloom.*
> *He was waiting for you to bloom. Oh! Love yourself!*
>
> *Said the Black Child: Love me, I love you;*
> *you will breathe the black aromas of my body;*
> *you will drink the black blood of my veins*
> *from the red wound of my mouth;*
> *love me, I love you; you will kiss my black fleeces.*
>
> *Said the Black Child: Oh! Come drown*
> *in the black lake of my adamantine eyes;*
> *I will hide you there; where you*
> *can sleep forever calm in the black night of Nothingness*
> *which I have vowed to you, since I love you*
>   *Me, the Black Child.*
>   *Ah!—Alas!—Ah!—Ah!*

And his fingers choked from the strings a kind of sob, where kisses were dying in agony.

The King had become very pale. Very pale, of the same pallor of the indecisive mist of light that now tarnished the stained glass window. The lamps were extinguished: large wings of shadow fell from the tops of the trenches inlaid with gold; the royal curtains were deepened with black folds; it was a heavy, cold sepulchral vault that seemed to support the large Jewish columns.

And the King seemed to fall asleep, his head dipped in the cushions.

However, he asked, in a voice that was far away:

"Where did you learn this song?"

"Master, I have only known it from this day that has just finished. A woman was singing it near the silver gate. I have been told that she has wandered there for nights, asking for the King."

"You saw this woman?"

"Master, at dusk I was near the gate. She was seated on a coping of brass. She has eyes that are two furnaces of shadow; in her tawny hair there are white bristles and she cried while she looked at me. She said: 'I would like to see the King.' Then she sang and got up to leave, desperate, and crying. She was black sorrow in the pink of sunset. She did not say her name, but I knew they must leave the city at dawn. They go to unknown countries, beyond the lakes, behind the infinite deserts; to countries where there are marvelous cities with palaces of solid gold, with topaz domes, with flags flying on bronze masts in the splendor of safety. They will come out, this dawn, through the Stone Gate."

The King said: "Go away and be silent."

✳

The wings of shadow had fallen back. Curtains with royal blossoms and great sacred symbols awoke the flamboyance of their rare fabrics. Confused noises rose from the countryside. On the river, enslaved fishermen sang. The red sails looked like wings of blood. From the tops of the terraces, the beating of copper discs announced the day.

Then the king wanted to put on his pompous clothes: over his sun-colored dress, where pentacles displayed their magical sanctity; over his robe with the quadrangled garlands of lotus in sardonyx; he set his ceremonial gorget, some light and divine work of a goldsmith, all trellised with precious stones; and the sparkling tiara on his forehead.

He appeared on the eastern terrace at the same time as the sun appeared behind the distant hills.

From there, one dominated the whole valley: first the massive ramparts, then the wide, peaceful river, then the giant greens of the royal parks and, further on, expanses of chalky plains, stained with gray grasses and closed by a low wall of blue hills.

The walls of the palace ran crookedly along the rock, from distance to distance, flanked by enormous and ugly square towers. And at the bottom, on the left, the Stone Gate pierced a colossal cube with a crenellated top.

51

It was a dawn of Cimmerian peace that refreshes thought.

There, on the white road, on the dry road where the caravans go, a troop of wanderers, wagons, horsemen and a black line of cattle . . . and behind, lingering in constant regret, with eyes turned toward the palace, a woman. She, the little slave formerly beloved, now aged, but still beautiful as a savage lioness.

She saw the King: he was alone, standing on the stone parapet above the abyss, alone in his majesty as Man-God, his head crowned with stars.

Tears burned his eyes, ran down his cheeks, stopped in his immaculate beard. She must have seen them from a distance, like precious stones fallen from his tiara.

The sun, already high, made an apotheosis. The mandrakes exuded troubling fervor. But she was no more than a black spot, almost invisible on the distant road, an atom of lost love . . .

The magical song vibrated in the listening air, but so weak, so vague, as if in a voice from the infinite. But the King, however, heard it as very close to him, distinct and living, with inflections that crushed his heart, and he thought he saw her eyes shine there, like two fallen stars.

HOMECOMING

For Raoul Pascalis.

WITH a chance encounter, on a day last summer, Life brought together two whom it had separated for eight years.

A supreme joy overwhelmed their hearts with fertile blood, joyful in a germination of hope. For, despite the fact that in the souls of both the ardor of old had been perpetuated, they had painfully believed each had forgotten the other.

She was crossing a deserted street, under a warm afternoon sky. She was alone; he passed: in his chest great blows beat tumultuously, and when, turning away, he saw her continue her slow way, a red rage stopped him. A chorus of regret stifled, from his funeral lament, the vibrant light in which she walked.

Alone!

At the courtyard of a church, the young girl seemed to wait. He looked at her from afar, still hesitating, torn in the hollow of his stomach by too much emotion.

Alone!

And it was She! She seemed taller, more dark-haired, her gait weary and broken.

On an imperceptible sign from her parasol, he ventured a few steps, but she crossed the religious threshold. He followed her. Among the darkness of the vaults, still blinded by the sun, he had to look for a moment; almost wishing she was no longer there, so close was he to fainting, his throat strangled with love and too many words that tore at his lips and which he would not dare, could not say.

On her knees, she tilted her head in her hands. And to see her so close to him, after so many hours of tears and desires and all the torture of doubt, was like his life's blood halting with a sharp pain, a dizzying whirl of everything around him: a statue of Saint-Pierre on an altar . . . the pulpit of marble with bas-reliefs of false gold . . . and those theological virtues made of painted plaster which supported it . . . and through the air, crumbling from the ceiling, fell the light from an enormous rose window . . .

A few moments: centuries of agitated waiting, dizzying anguish, spasmodic fever, and all his being stiffened, invaded by terror. What would she say? What would she do? Did she even know that he had followed her? Had she even recognized him? Eight years! Could she still remember? My God! Their old kisses . . . their oaths . . . their foolishness (she, sixteen, he, nineteen!), the daily letters, their meetings everywhere, in the crowds, in the theater, in the church; the two months living together . . . all their hours lived side by side . . . and their embraces . . . and all, all the past! Could she still remember . . . ?

Three o'clock struck. Footsteps in a nave, the white surplice of a priest between the columns, a confessional door which opens, closes quickly, and then the slipping noise of the wicket, the whispering of confessions in a low voice, in the silent shadows.

He summoned the courage to come near her. She heard the sound of his footsteps on the flagstones and lifted her head slowly: her eyes were full of tears. Through these tears she looked at him, beautiful with happy pain, with one word on her lips, barely murmured: "Always."

The next day, through the lonely roads of this suburb devoured by sun and dust, a cab carried them. The reflection of the blinds filled the rolling chamber with blue lights, enveloping them in an atmosphere of fairyland.

For a long time they remained silent, like two who are strangers, who have nothing to say to each other.

She spoke first, hesitantly:

"The place . . . the place on my neck . . . you remember . . ."

He kissed her neck, voraciously, but she freed herself. Then he took her hands and began to look at her, kneeling before her:

"It's you . . . yes, it's you . . . your eyes . . . your lips . . . your ears . . . and your fingers . . ."

He covered them with caresses. She was content to answer with a languid smile:

"Yes . . . you see . . . it's me . . . always the same . . ."

Against the girl's breast he furtively rested his head, distraught. He murmured:

"You thought you were forgotten . . . and me?"

She repeated her promises:

"No, I will never marry . . . I want to only have belonged to you . . . to you alone . . . just to you . . ."

He could scarcely hear her, as if he had suddenly been borne away from her, and he began to cry. He cried for a long time. The sensation of passing minutes escaped him: he was lost on a dry plain, as a bloody sun set. To the very edge of the horizon was an immovable sea of stones and dead grasses, battered by funereal hues. He wandered alone; a feverish thirst burned him; he heard the sound of approaching springs, not far from him, and he bent down to drink, but the water suddenly dried up and his damnation began again. "Here is my heart," he said to himself, and a trembling hand took his, and a worried voice asked, "Why are you crying?"

"It's happiness," he answered, pulling himself together; and the falsity of these words revolted him. It was a lie to all he had felt for an hour, while everything was striving to destroy him; a lie to the happiness he had dreamed of, in finding her again. In vain he exhausted himself in expressing the mortal emotion whose hope, alone, for years, had made him faint.

He tried a litany of memories:

"Do you remember our first meeting?"

"Yes, I had just been so sick . . . I was very pale . . . you looked at me in such a strange way . . . as with pity . . ."

"And our bench, there, in the park . . ."

"And the day of our first embrace . . . Yes, the furnished room . . . I was ashamed . . . but I loved you so much . . ."

"And when you thought you were pregnant . . ."

"I would have killed myself . . . surely . . ."

In spite of himself he clasped her in his arms, at the thought that she might have died thus because of him, for him, left him indifferent and tortured at the same time. The impulses of old, their failing only to look at each other from afar, the mad happiness he had felt at touching a fold of her dress, his vertigo of intoxication when she rested her head on his shoulder, all these he persisted in evoking. A sort of contempt for her, for him, rather, to see her there, in the blue light of that equivocal box of love . . . He wanted to make her suffer, he would have liked to, himself, suffer more than he did, but his will failed. He had come to surrender his soul, his heart, his desires, as in the past, sincerely, and everything in his gestures and words seemed to him false. It was becoming a dreadful torture. Oh, the lie of the lips, the sterility of words and appearances! The being overflowing with tenderness, the nerves bursting to break with contented joy, the head blazing with so many ardent memories! The tongue dries up, the voice rattles in the throat, as if all inside, deep inside, were dead. The ashes of the past smother you; there is between these two bodies which once were one, all irrevocable oblivion . . . Life has deformed them, the image is not the same one, where one once rested his softened looks, and rancor awakens from the mutual sufferings that were imposed.

However, he tried to make an effort against himself. He began to look at her again. She seemed less slender.

Her once-blonde hair had turned brown, and her complexion, once so pious, with such delicate sad pallor, revealed now too much health and vigor. The frail, light flower of flesh had blossomed into violent perfumes. She kissed him on the lips, but that deep kiss, which had lately thrown him to the abyss of vertiginous love, now almost revolted him. He turned his head away sharply, pushed aside the mad mouth with a blunt gesture. On the girl's face a mask of excruciating pain dropped, and from her discolored lips, all throbbing with chills, these words fell quietly:

"You do not love me anymore."

He did not dare to answer anything. She would not understand! "No," he repeated to himself, "I do not love you anymore. I do not love you anymore as I see you today, no. But I still love you through the image of the one you once were, that you will never be again. I love your memory, the distant reality of you, of which you offer me only the fallen shadow. Perhaps you have remained the same after all, and it is I who cannot recognize you, but what does it matter, since you appear to me different and removed from the old splendor? . . . So stay alive in the sepulcher of my memory, in the beauty of your past form . . . for I cannot find it in your present form."

They did not exchange any more words. The minutes flowed slowly; and they had the sensation of being shut up for eternity in the silence of the rolling box, among the blue lights of the blinds. Both there for eternity, with the weight of their cursed love on their hearts, and all their miserable lovers' flesh torn apart by the harrow of regret . . .

LORD SORRY

For Henry Bauer

THE following item appeared in the newspapers a few days ago:

> *Last night at the Folies-Bergère, at the moment when Loïe Fuller took the stage, a dreadful incident occurred which greatly impressed the spectators.*
>
> *A young man, occupying the No. 22 orchestra chair, suddenly collapsed, uttering a loud cry. Help was immediately dispensed; first aid was given by Dr. L—— who was in the room. Documents found on the man established his identity. His name was Lord Sorry, twenty-seven years of age, and his residence was at the Grand Hotel, where he was transported and where he died two hours later, succumbing to an essential encephalitis. The police commis-*

Lord Sorry! These three syllables rang in my memory like a knell. "Lord Sorry! Lord Sorry!" I repeated; and confused memories stirred in me, a portrait seen once . . . mysterious stories in which a character of the same name had been the hero . . . and the resemblance of a man who, in the seat beside mine for several evenings at the Music Hall in rue Richer, to this portrait? A strange character with a disturbing look, he shook with nervous tic and, as soon as the magic dancer appeared among the polychromatic smoke of the spotlights, he panted and gnashed his teeth . . . I saw, in the dim light, how he wrung his hands. When the show finished I watched him leave, staggering, clinging to the backs of the chairs, the edge of the boxes, and an usherette I questioned told me that he had been there every night to see Loïe Fuller, and that one evening he had suffered a seizure. "A fit of nerves . . . convulsions . . . many grimaces!"

I suddenly remembered. Yes, Lord Sorry, who had been maddened with shrill sensations, a frenetic voluptuousness that had produced the most subtle and the most costly fantasies of art, who, all that last *season*, had been the scandalous chronicle of London . . . Lord Sorry! It was him! Undoubtedly, it could only be him, that model for the portrait which now came back to me in its capricious attractiveness. I was sure of it now. We almost met one day in Whistler's studio, where he was completing a sitting . . . and suddenly my impressions of that time were completely clear.

A pure masterpiece, that canvas, where Whistler had immortalized the features of the young Lord with his prodigious powers of evocation! Sitting on a high chair, Lord Sorry stood out in profile, in the familiar pose of that famous portrait of Carlyle by the same master artist. The falling hands testified to the weariness of the effort, a nonchalance, a need for rest from the gesture that was supremely aristocratic. He was dressed with a mysterious and complicated elegance, an obscure indifference, no more jewelry than a platinum snake on his left wrist. And his whole being seemed dismal and ghostly on that glaucous background o aquamarine, vaguely lit with dead reflections.

But the face . . . oh, that flaming face of madness with the pale blush of Velasquez's *Philip IV* on the cheekbones, and that discolored blond hair . . . the huge lower jaw, an anthropoid chin, adding brutality to a sickly being . . . and the upper part of the face, in contrast, a noble, swollen forehead of the ideal. And the smoldering glow of the delirium from beyond in the depths of those colorless eyes. An intense soul lived there, haughty, secretly enclosed in the esotericism of his dreams, sheltered from the usual obsessions. And the entire portrait gained a special life from its dreary harmony of warm gray and ardent blacks, a melancholy life amidst an atmosphere of wings broken in haughty plunges onto the shores of fantasy, but reaching only a translucent wall of slumbering water lit by faded gleams.

Expressing my admiration for the portrait, Whistler had told me about the model. There was, among other tales, the story of a streetwalker picked up in the slums of London with whom Lord Sorry had lived for four years. Behind walls legendarily frescoed, in a strange house of pale floral tapestries and bright lacquered furnishings, she spent her indolent days, dressed in floating silks. Only walking or resting under the fresh green glow of stained-glass windows, she was eternally virginal in the young grace of her form, the complex and rare harmony of her lines.

On certain days, the white floors of the hall were strewn with stemmed flowers. From the top of a golden balcony she radiantly leaned, like "The Blessed Damozel" of the divine Rossetti whose "eyes were deeper than the depth of waters stilled at even; she had three lilies in her hand, and the stars in her hair, which was like ripe corn, were seven . . ."

From the thousands of her nocturnal race Lord Sorry had elected her, seemingly at random and without concern for her infamous and miserable past, not with the hope of sensual joys more learned or more servile, which would have guided so many other men, but only because she possessed the ideal profile, the soulful eyes, the restless languor in pose and gesture of the young women in Burne Jones' *Mirror of Venus*. There were months of unbearable exile, when no exterior distractions were allowed, lost in the depths of his remote and private park, alone with the presence of a living masterpiece. Did he love her? And with what kind of love? He never consented to the baseness of possessing her physically: it was enough that she live her life in the silent splendor of a dream of accomplished art.

But one day the dream collapsed, and he sent the girl away laden with gold, and had the strange house knocked down to the last stone so that nothing could remain of this illusory past.

As my memories unfolded, it became clear that the Lord Sorry of Whistler's portrait could only be the Lord Sorry of the Folies Bergère. But what additional detail had I missed? . . . And I remembered the response of the usherette: Lord Sorry came there every night, *every night*, to see Loïe Fuller perform. I saw him sitting next to me, in the grip of an ecstatic crisis. I heard his panting breath. I could see him wringing his hands.

For this unsatisfied, unknowable soul who perpetually thirsted for new vibrations, from the very first day that this mysterious and maddening vision had appeared to him she must have signified a fatal end of an obsession, an inexorable possession.

Among the undulating whorls of her turning veils— the bloody petals of a huge living orchid, the rolling waves of pearly foam, the beating wings of a gigantic butterfly studded with iridescent green eyes, all those soft, opalescent powders and fabulous swarms of shining reptile scales—he must have been carried away by the enjoyment of supernatural vertigo. A dangerous voluptuousness for those sick sensations showed on his face, for an organism like his own, shaken by all the excess of fictitious excitement which he had been heedlessly indulging in for years, was demented . . . and no doubt, as well, she communicated with him, that demoniac dancer who throbbed with the desires of the crowd surrounding him, a whole crowd charging the weakened, ultra-sensitive Lord Sorry with its unhealthy electricity. No doubt she evoked, in her flowering of petals, a poisonous blossom with murderous pollen; in her dance of flashing wings the image of the Atropos, the death's head sphinx; in her grappling with the scaled rings, the shape of the Serpent with a thousand heads on which reposes Shiva, the god of destruction. And also, there was the flesh of a woman, the living, warm, complex flesh of a woman, the mystery of her sex appeared in these haunting incarnations! Does she not symbolize the eternal attraction of mystery through the basest realities? Perhaps an enigma is agitated in her, whose truth will remain forever ignored, an enigma of Rhythm and Color still unfathomed? A nightmare ghost in a haunted room—the burial chamber where the agony of this century rattles—it seems a curse springs from her. In the shadows of nothingness from which it suddenly arises, under the all-powerful will of the projectors that create it, it is as if a breath of madness, a hot whirlwind of delirium, irresistibly carries you away.

Lord Sorry was her first victim.

THE DAMSEL WITH THE LITTLE RED BALLOON

For Aurélien Scholl.

ALL frail, with the air of a convalescent flower, and so delicately sad amidst the noisy gaiety of the City, at the end of the day, she passed . . .

In her virginal white dress of tissue with mauve purple marks, a wide black surah corset raising her young breasts, her thin arms lost in the large, floating sleeves, but the rest of her body too indiscreetly molded in a flat skirt, she walked through the streets, a pretty form of half-mourning, sensual boredom.

The little red balloon fluttered, attached to the tip of her finger, like a bleeding heart. A symbol perhaps of some hurt love, in search of consoling caresses, or, simply the floating flag of an attentive mother, concerned with economic toys . . .

Eight days in a row, three months ago, then two days again just last week, I had the chance of meeting her.

At the same time of day, at the same corner of the same avenue.

It was one of those pale skies, a sweet, late-summer sky of wise light. The air carries too much heavy tenderness, moving through the crowd like a happy lassitude; and one goes, totally at peace, exaggeratedly sensitive. In the branches of chestnut trees, there is a green revival of late leaves.

Beautiful days conducive to fertile imaginations, subtle tenderness!

The Damsel appeared.

Did she pretend to ignore me or to recognize me? We greeted each other with a glance. The little balloon fidgeted, and as she came against the setting sun, a little red lit up her pale cheeks. Quickly she turned her head away, but a smile still lingered on her lips, and, feverishly, she amused herself by nibbling the purple tulle of her veil.

Her emotion exalted me.

"Damsel," thought I, "how much I would like the right to love you, and to tell you, for the delicious trouble which I feel you are in, you seem to me so different today from the dream that I created of you when contemplating your walk on the days of our first meetings! There are indeed some of your guises (those resigned nods of your head, the touching indecision of your step . . . and the vivid flight of the red balloon!) that I can again find— but with how much more abandonment, with how much more considerate suppleness! I tremble, it is true, to set foot in the closed garden of your soul. But to what good, alas! If you knew! A thousand words spoken, would they ever be worth the deep and almost too abundant confidence of your lips, which avenge themselves on that purple veil?"

I followed the little red balloon. Sometimes, in the evening breezes, it pretended to be struggling, impatient for freedom, and quickly she brought it close to her, fearfully. Sometimes, with the rate of a slow march, it hovered over her head, very calm, between the clear wings of her hat.

For a moment I thought I was losing her. My heart began to beat, and I felt an icy squeeze at the nape of my neck. My thoughts distressed me: "Yes, it's over! Never again will I see the Damsel with the little red balloon!" The warm charm of that end of day, so finely luminous, cast me into a strange fever. "No longer to see the Damsel with the little red balloon . . . !" A lamentable horizon of hours of mourning, of dark moral misery unfolded before me . . . if this happiness was taken from me . . .

But I saw her again!

At the entrance to a passage, a ragged little girl was parading a display of glittering trinkets. On her board, a tribe of little monkeys in red, green, yellow, blue chenille were agitated, as if alive. Some danced on brass threads; others rode a bicycle; some fought duels; many brandished tiny brooms. The Damsel had stopped, seduced, had chosen two she clipped to the folds of her belt, like two flowers . . . and went on her way.

Anticipating her movements, I dared to get a better look at her. A strange flame flickered in her eyes and her tired eyelids were shadowed—with too many dreams . . . or too much love?—which told me she was ardent and adventurous.

Where had she come from? Barely out of an embrace, still hot from a caress . . . and what caresses!

Where was she going? Ah! Her dreams, her life, the desires that swelled in her chest . . . would it be possible for me to know them?

"So many things about you," I continued, "Damsel, must they remain unknown to me? I am thirsty, yes, to possess you . . . Oh, not your young flesh as I feel, notwithstanding its ardor, that it is too ingenuous, but the divine in yourself, your dear thought, your dear little soul . . ."

She stopped again. In a glittering photographer's showcase stall portraits of half-naked actresses offered poses, beauties in vogue, highly rated, all on a background of gold tint.

She stared at them for a long time, alas! A frown of sadness and envy on her forehead, jealous of their triumph. This weakness distressed me. What, that was her conception of life, her dream of happiness? Such vulgar appetites could really fill that charming head?

So, then, it was pleasing to lower her to the level of the others, and even lower, to trivialize her, to degrade her. I drew from it the pleasure of a form of revenge against myself. I was just about to retrace my steps when she turned her head away from the showcase, as if she had guessed what she was doing to me, and with an infinitely moved, infinitely contrite look, she seemed to beg, "Oh! Do not judge me . . . Believe me, I'm better . . . much better . . . and forgive me! . . . come, and you will know . . ."

At nightfall, we arrived in the depths of a lost district, in a square of meager trees and marble statues among yellowed lawns, a place of fresh air and cleanness among the high gray houses.

A mist of indecisive light still stained the sky. The alleys of the garden were deserted and the Damsel hastened her pace. In the silence, the slight rustling of her dress on the sand and, still, the flight of the little balloon, barely red in the extinguishing light.

I wanted to join her, but she sensed my presence and suddenly ran.

A rustic bridge connected the two banks of an artificial lake, and there cascades of rockery lamented a ridiculous complaint from murky water.

She ran. A few steps further on, from the bench where he was sitting, an old man stood up, lamentable in his faded frock-coat, a thin phantom of misery who waved his arms in the void. His arms were long, very long, and his hands, the hands of a child, were gesticulating towards the Damsel.

Quickly, she joined him. He was overcome with joy. She gave to him the little balloon, and the two chenille monkeys, and he pressed them against his heart, uttering chuckles: "Oh! Pretty, pretty!" And he covered the face of the Damsel with greedy kisses.

Then they left. I saw them from far away, very slowly the old man leaned on the girl's arm; she supported his faltering steps. And all around, over the stunted trees, over the vaguely white form of the marbles, over the dry grass, over the black water, the night extended its cover of shadow.

"Oh, Damsel!" I thought. "Why have you so misunderstood? Please give me alms and lend an ear to my repentance. In me you will remain a memory of the most delicate devotion, and of so many minutes of the most exquisite sentimental enthusiasm I've ever known. You, who know so well how to relieve the ineluctable distress of old men, what balm could you have shed on the wounds of my poor heart . . . I miss you . . ."

IRON WIRE

For Mlle. A. L.

WE called her Iron Wire because of her extreme thinness; a charming, not morbid, emaciation, that she wore with a strange grace, a rare and irresistible seductiveness. I can still see her fine head with her too-large eyes perpetually lit by her sparkling spirit that knew how to be painfully tender in the face of any vision of sadness, her pale lips drawn into a melancholy smile and her entire face suffused with an air of severe resignation and supplicating passivity. On her forehead there was a tuft of blonde hair, floating and disorganized, which she obstinately tried to smooth with a familiar gesture of her slender fingers. The rest of her body, a gangly skeleton like the carcass of a little cuckoo bird, was always clasped in narrow, transparent robes, signaling her loose and inconsistent person.

Among the heavy boredom and gross monotony of our student life in that small city of Provence, where the austere traditions of the seventeenth-century cities of magistracy are held under the supervision of the ridiculously grave and solemn nobility of the gown, Iron Wire uttered, in her frank gaiety and capricious indifference, the craziness of her twenty years.

Poor little Iron Wire! With her pretty, boyish nature and her amicable indifference, she possessed a heart capable of full devotion and abnegation; and all of us had been cared for, watched over, and pampered by her through our hours of sickness or spleen. And what an excellent adviser, loyal and simple, always on the side of the weak against the strong, wielding a male straightness despite her disheveled logic! But she was stubborn, stubborn with a dry, animal obstinacy against which all reasoning, as well as all violence (and all tenderness), remained powerless. Once set, by the least of challenges or for the most futile fantasy, no human will would have been able to tame her obstinacy. She opposed with a quiet energy, a calm firmness which broke any resistance, and her weak being was suddenly endowed with a formidable robustness, as if possessed by a foreign force rightfully installed in her for her defense, and while she could be broken, she was never defeated. But as soon as the crisis had passed, she was the first to laugh at herself in a fit of sudden jest, with two tears welling up in a blossoming of emotion, and it was over.

At the time I knew "Iron Wire," she had been for two years the mistress of a student, Louis Renouard, with whom I quickly shared one of those delicate and lasting sympathies that come rather from the head than from the heart. It remains, in my memory, my first deep friendship.

He was three years younger than I and, from the day we met, I held a kind of enthusiastic admiration for my new friend. He was of both a shy and violent character, bringing to all he did an abundant and passionate soul, while I myself was then undergoing a dreadful torture of intellectual drought and lack of moral interest which desolated my youth. So, Louis Renouard appeared to me as a providential example. It was also the first time I had been able to live in the company of a woman other than my mother, or my sisters and their friends, and so Iron Wire became another link attaching me to Renouard.

All three of us spent long, familiar evenings together, as they lived a little outside the small town, not far from the train station, whose perpetual movements filled the air with the roar of life. Their windows opened onto the fields and our interminable conversations before the clear dusk of summer twilights, where so many things speak of infinity around you, were sweet to me. As to me (or as to us, I should say, to acknowledge Iron Wire) Louis Renouard professed a sort of protective benevolence, delicately discreet. We were both "his spiritual children," as he willingly called us, and we listened to him with a religious respect. I owe him my sentimental salvation, for he taught me the science of exalting myself, but without any systematic drought of being, and in the most fruitful and broadest way. As for Iron Wire: gifted as she was with that supple nature which we knew, save for her stubbornness which would prove fatal and which my friend confessed himself powerless to cure, no doubt she had become the most exquisite and most precious of women.

But he himself, Louis Renouard, through what passionate dramas, by what painful steps had he drawn such an early experience of life and its mystery? And how, instead of letting himself down, had it become possible for him to draw from them such a complete and beautiful teaching? This is what I still wonder when, often, I think back on the past.

"Suffer," he would repeat; "become accustomed to finding in the world, every minute, a reason for suffering. Suffer everything, from the brightness of the sun which symbolizes the gross exuberance, the cheap glamour of most men; suffer from the splendor of flowers, perfumes and colors; suffer from the divine music and sumptuous poems where the frantic hearts of artists are wounded daily for us, at every minute of the hour, like the blood of Christ. Torture yourself happily, like the ascetics, under the iron lash of the hair shirt; flagellate yourself with imaginary disciplines under your hood of disdain and disgust for the usual joys on which the humanity of barbarians, which we are, feeds; let the invisible tears of your heart flow. It is with suffering alone that you will come to know yourself, to possess yourself, to divide what you contain of the divine and the ideal. Then, from that blood, from those tears with which you have quenched the earth, you will one day witness a surge—great, strong, and adorned with all the magnificence of the eternal flowers—of the miraculous blossoming of You. Then you will truly be a man, that is to say, a small piece of the throbbing soul of the world, and you will enjoy the joy of living."

When Louis Renouard became silent, Iron Wire and I, as recollection extolled us to the sound of those words, would both advance: I to shake his hand gratefully, she kissing his forehead, taking his head in her hands and covering it with happy tears. She had many of those spontaneous movements, full of simple ardor, where one felt that she gave herself up entirely, body and soul, no longer anything human or inferior surviving in her. At those times, something of heaven descended into this nervous little girl full of voluntary caprices and mischievous gaiety, and transfigured her. She became the sister of the great holy mystics, visionaries and ecstatics who, in their transports, touch the threshold of the gardens of paradise.

During the whole second summer of our relationship, Renouard, Iron Wire and I became accustomed to transporting the intimacy of our daily chats into the countryside. We had an early dinner and found ourselves outside the city, beside an old doorway, at dusk. The charm of those walks has remained in my mind, moving and sweet as some forgotten perfumes that we rediscover one day long after, in passing, and in which a whole piece of our life remains bound.

For the year I had been receiving Renouard's friendly lessons, my dryness of soul had been fertilized little by little. Instead of the gray discouragement, the dull indifference with which I had unnecessarily suffered so much, I felt my vision of the world enriching from day to day, and rejoiced to attribute all the merit to my friend. As for "Iron Wire," a change had also taken place in her; insensibly, her stubborn fits were becoming rarer and Renouard and I never ceased to congratulate ourselves, unaware of the terrible and inescapable denial she was soon to give us.

One evening when I was waiting for them, instead of the usual rendezvous, Louis Renouard came alone. I had the presentiment of a misfortune. I went to meet him.

"And Iron Wire?" I asked anxiously.

"Alas! My dear friend, you will not see her tonight. I had to leave her in penance. But rest assured, she runs no danger. I am trying to definitively cure her ugly defect, which you know about, with a supreme attempt. We will go and deliver her in a moment, Yes, just as we were going out to join you she suddenly, stubbornly, chose, from some futile motive, a blue ribbon to tie about her neck, while, to me, a pink ribbon seemed more of a fit . . . that's it, I think. Then, as I was afraid of making you wait, and she persisted in not wanting to follow me, I locked her in her room."

"Have you really done that?" I exclaimed. "But with her excited nature, with that madness that takes her when she's in such a nervous state . . ."

He interrupted me dryly:

"I beg you not to interfere with her. We will go at once and deliver her, in an hour or so. This is the deadline that I set myself.

Alas! How long this walk by the roads devoured by shadow seemed to me. We scarcely uttered ten words, and in what voices of anxiety, for I felt that Renouard shared my own fears.

At last, half-past nine struck from the bell tower of the cathedral.

"We can go back," he said. "Accompany me. 'Iron Wire' will be pleased to see you."

Poor little Iron Wire! When we entered the room, a horrible sight made us recoil. She lay stretched out on the ground, groaning with a death rattle, covered with blood and disfigured. At her temples deep holes were hollowed out, from which flowed all her frail life. And her small bird's body crushed by death, had her arms folded over her chest, squeezing her exhaling heart . . . and her ruffled blonde hair was soiled with blood . . .

The room was in an inexpressible disorder. Stains of blood were everywhere, on the furniture, on the bed where she had rolled, and at the corner of the marble fireplace was a burst of red flesh, sticky with hair and a scrap of brains.

We carried her to her bed. She died a few moments later without uttering a word. Her gaze enveloped us one last time, with a look of tenderness and pardon, then it was over.

She was buried the next day. Many of us followed her procession, and when the coffin was lowered into the grave, it looked like a coffin for a child, a little girl, covered entirely under white flowers.

As for Louis Renouard, he went insane, eight days later, from desperate remorse. He had to be interned at the hospice at Montdevergues, near Avignon, where he still lives.

THE WATCH

For Claudius Blanc.

NOTHING is more fatal to me than the return of blue skies.

As a child, I needed days to accustom my eyes to the spring light. I experienced strange troubles. Really, I was as afraid of the sun as of an inexorable enemy. Its rays tore my eyelids, and hurt my soul. The warmth of the air choked me. The revival of things around me led me to revolt. What a joy to tear the young buds, to kill these spikes of life just born . . . to avenge myself on the flowers, since the sun was too far away!

Since then, never better than in those days, have I felt the bitterness of existing, the inanity of all effort, the eternal escape of memory to the common grave of oblivion. Ah! Those hasty spring days, they filled me with such an inexpressible distress! The flow of sap that begins to swell the world cries loudly of the death of all in us, and those breaths laden with wandering life, do they not carry the ashes of the past? A past which ceases to be mine and becomes impersonal, that of another, known long ago, which told me stories now forgotten. Scattered shreds of our life make up the swarms of coursing atoms.

But the sun that I flee, this pale sun of renewals, so soft and caressing through the blue of the atmosphere when the last fresh breezes pass, this sun that I hate—yes, that I hate—it attracts me, nevertheless, with an irresistible seduction. To see it play behind my curtains, to see it slip like liquid along my windows in a joyful flow, to see it infiltrate, timidly, into the house—it seems to me that it calls me, with an infinitely fine voice, capable of enough tenderness to appease the perpetual anguish of my nerves . . . and even though I remember the wounds it inflicted upon me, its treachery, its vengeance, our whole past of common hatred, in spite of myself I must go out to drink it, to breathe it, to hear it, to feel it enter into my being by all the pores, as if it were the most subtle poison . . .

I went to bed very early that evening, after hours and hours of dangerous strolling among the light and the buds and because, at the end of the dinner, I was overwhelmed by weariness (a drunken rolling was in the depths of my skull, my arms and legs were like cotton, I was unable to make a gesture, seize an object or take a step), but I woke up in the middle of the night.

To the ends of my fingers, to the tips of my hair, a soothing freshness held me, like after the diffusion of an injection of morphine. It was the same super-acuity of perception, the same frenetic exaltation of sensitivity (while also a kind of numbness) that makes you a docile slave, a passive toy of appearances, and which exasperates realities and disfigures them.

A rhythmic, imperceptible noise, unbelievably regular, spurred my attention: it seemed like mechanical works, with a wooden heart, echoed by fibers of sound. "Where can this be coming from? Where does it really occur? Or is it here, in my brain, behind the cranial septum? Here?" And I touched my left temple with one finger, so much did I feel that a worm was spinning inside me, a worm armed with a tiny tool whose regulating wheel was obstinately ticking. Yet I listened, holding my breath, as if the noise was outside.

Despite the darkness, it occurred to me to take my watch and look at the time it was supposed to be, and my questions faded away: Had I been mad, that I'd not realized it sooner? *Parbleu!* The tool that twisted my skull was only the vibration of the movement of the watch on my night stand. I rested it in its place and, tranquilized, tried to go back to sleep. In vain. The noise was growing, growing, the inevitable rhythm of seconds pounded by a gigantic pendulum. And suddenly I was afraid. I was frozen with the idea that I was eternally condemned to endure this noise that inexorably disintegrated my life. And then, everywhere, always, this obsession would possess me. I tried superhuman efforts to focus my will power on other thoughts, but only one image came up: a park full of sunshine, overflowing with sap, under a blue arch of the sky like an abyss. Before my dazzled eyes a vision then sprang up, of such intensity that it recreated again that accursed reality. That spring landscape, where all day I had wandered imprudently, appeared immediately. The buds were bursting; a delirium of life shook the branches; the air carried fiery emanations, and the sun above, in an immaculate azure, poured its rain of seed.

And the noise was still growing . . . always growing. Then, with a gesture of rage, I grabbed my watch and threw it to the end of the room, far away, away from me . . . there was the splintering of broken glass . . . and I thought everything was over.

But the noise became formidable. In my brain, the regular breathlessness of a steam engine's piston shots began to beat. Whistling jets filled my brain; in the interlobar grooves, large gears armed with tapered blades rolled, regulating the perpetual coming and going of the unleashed rhythm. At the stroke of seconds, the walls of my cranial box were dislocated. The sutures were going to snap . . .

How long did it take? How many minutes, how many centuries? Consciousness escapes me. I remember, however, that I jumped down from my bed, and I fell to the floor, seeking in the darkness the instrument of demon torture, the cursed watch, and having finally found it, I threw it in the street through the opened window . . . I remember that. But I also remember that the noise only increased. The enormous clamor mingled with the murmur of the sap laboring among the trees. Its lightning-fast growth rose to the sun and descended in its rays. Life and Time were no more than the one, the only, the all-powerful force that begets and kills . . . and I, caught in their whirlwind, swept away like a wisp, was crumbling into the abyss of madness, where this infernal obsession has followed me since . . .

THE BEGGAR

For Stéphane Mallarmé.

IN my hours of revolt against life, its injustice and its complaisance, in these crises of moral fluctuation where one also feels seduced by the fallacious mirage of the Best and the Worst, sterile sophisms, nasty compromises, and all the horde of small, easy to commit crimes that sometime assail you, too deliciously tempting . . . a benevolent image comes to visit me, whose eyes suddenly illuminate my conscience. Phantom of sweetness, of divine resignation, of high wisdom, her memory remained alive in my soul after so many years, and in spite of the perpetual influx of impressions on my sensibility. From her lips fall, like a precious dew, the words of indulgence and pardon; it is enough for me to see her appear, animated suddenly by the life of my memory, for the black veil of selfishness and indifference, through which I once gazed at the spectacle of the world, to part. A superhuman charm transfigures this pale face of a human being far away, a being over there, at the very bottom of the enclosure of light where we had known each other, an unreachable form caught in the current of reminiscences. And here, I am again the too-pensive child that I was, the creature of simplicity and ignorance that the fever of living has withered.

Ah! Dear, good beggar, your lessons remain precious to me, and I like to evoke you as a poor, sickly flower, whose perfume speaks of death, bent over my ardor of a young growth swollen with too abundant sap.

In the large enclosure where our childish games were played, a beggar came every day. Very small and bent in two by old age, smaller indeed than the smallest of us, the eldest of which was scarcely twelve, she leaned on an emaciated parasol. Dressed in a black woolen ruffle with a brightly colored scarf around her waist, and her tousled dry gray hair encircling her forehead with a crown of revolt, she presented the living form from poor fairy tales, of curse throwers and child snatchers. The color of her eyes especially terrified us: they were yellow, the yellow of old gold glittering with red. Fixed on us, an infinite softness moistened them, but they were also stirring, animated, one might have said they were like crackling embers, voracious.

She had chosen as her usual seat a large stone among thistles and nettles, not far from the wall of dry earth which enclosed this kingdom of our games. Behind her, a constellation of great suns circled blindingly, and wild lilies grew by her side.

At first, instinctively, we were frightened by her misery, a repugnance separated us from her like our disgust at her sordid rags. However much our whole hearts urged us towards the poor woman sitting there, looking at us with her kind eyes, our hereditary contempt and the leavening of our very education made her odious and repulsive to us. Alas, until then we had been taught only conventional, mercenary pity, but the sublime flower of compassion which springs forth from the human being at the end of painful struggles had not yet taken root in our hearts. Alas! . . .

Gradually, however, an intimacy was established between the beggar and the children we were then. As soon as we saw her coming to the entrance of the enclosure, we rushed to meet her, help her walk . . . There was a jostling, and even blows, to choose whose shoulder would support her trembling hand. Was there an obscure feeling of pride, or an instinctive consciousness of her vigor and the years she had left, felt by childhood facing the weakness of the elders already marked by death? Regardless, we began to love her for her very misery, proud to help her and to pity her by feeling ourselves, all of us, safe from such destitution.

Once seated, she thanked us with a gesture and begged us not to worry about her, to resume our amusements. But our joy had ended. Her mere presence was enough to make us serious, to make our childish frivolities weigh against the impression of pain scattered over the world, of which the poor woman was a thrilling part. Then we grouped ourselves at her feet, as on the steps of a throne, and we contemplated her with respect. A generous exaltation carried us away, an enthusiasm to pity and admire her, a curiosity to find ourselves face to face with a being whose nature was different from ours, no doubt of another race, with the prestige of the past glorified lavishly in lamentable wrinkles on her pale face. How many things she might know! How many endless number of years had she lingered? And the mystery of her life seemed terrible to us . . . had the just cruelty of an expiation for crimes once committed bent her thus in two, made her lips tremble, lit her glance with those occasional flames? Was it terror, or was it only the fatality of existing too long and robbing others of the remainder of their lives, which stigmatized her fearful distress?

Some afternoons, she remained silent the entire time she was among us. Darkly, she remained there, motionless, abased in pain, tears flooding her face. At other times, on the contrary, a smile of fresh youth transfigured her, and she liked to tell us stories, to chat with our imaginations, intimately, finely, in an abandoned simplicity that delighted us. Ah, the beautiful and fruitful stories which our young hearts melted into! She spoke of the nobility of heroic devotion, of glorious kindness, the intoxicating splendor of the sufferings endured with resignation, the divine poetry of shared tears, and her voice became profound, supremely harmonious and sweet. The evening descended. Enraptured by the beggar's words, it seemed to us that the walls of the enclosure were crumbling; the landscape widened, in the dim light of the twilight the trees faded away, at the bottom of the enlarged sky a mist of low clouds was gilded at the top by the last rays of the sun, and above them, the heavens were unbounded.

A land of dreams was opening up, a land of brilliance and clarity peopled with charming beings, for the joy of whom all the treasures of life were scattered night and day. They drank the happiness of feeling simple and good from humble fountains. They picked tasty fruits from miracle orchards, fruits whose very hearts could not be bitter and that they ate smiling, in ecstasy. Some leaning on the arms of others, they wandered, beautifully happy, among the sympathy and fraternity of their fellows, and it seemed to us that little stars glittered on their foreheads.

The beggar continued to speak. Her voice, to our ears, had the sweetness of angelic harps. We looked at her. Her eyes were fixed on the sky, contemplating the same empire of happiness that she had just created for us with her mysterious lips. At last she rose. We walked her silently to the entrance onto the road, and for a long time our gazes followed her, fading in the shadows, carrying with her the beautiful mirage of our illusions.

Autumn came. The bloody sunsets filled the sky with wounds and the flaming clot of the sun rained red on a horizon of dead branches. A limitless despair had been tearing us all apart for eight days, because for a week the beggar had not reappeared. The thought of death, true destructive and inexorable death, assailed us, and we dared not even speak of the mysteriously absent one. Among the crumbling stones of the gap we bent each day, for hours, watching the road. The beggar did not return.

One evening, at last, she arrived, and our eyes exalted with joy and terror as we thought we were only seeing her ghost. She walked, dragging herself, smaller still, and we almost had to carry her to her usual place, as she staggered and we had to support her. With anxious tenderness we questioned her, but already she could no longer speak. The words whistled from her lips, as she lacked the strength to open her mouth and pronounce them, and the atrocious suffering, of not being able to say that which we so well felt that she meant, contracted her features, twisting her with revolted rage. All at once, however, she seemed to calm down, as if from a super-human effort. She opened her arms, and embraced us ardently. The evening breezes stirred the constellation of great suns behind her head; sobs shook us all and we felt faint with anguish and fear. Death was there, very near us, in the place of our games, we guessed. It was through the opening to the road that it must have entered our kingdom, and the frightful question arose: who of us would it strike?

For a long time we remained still, huddled against the body of the beggar, as in a citadel of compassion and gentleness where death could not reach us, daring no movement or word . . . until one of us, the oldest, the one who had just turned twelve, murmured:

"The beggar is dead."

And we all fled, running into the night.

THE PALE COUPLE

For Octave Mirbeau.

FROM the shadowy corner where a cigar glowed between two invisible lips, revealing the gold of a thick red mustache, redder at times than the ember, a tired voice begged:

"Would you like . . . a little music . . . Christiane . . . ?"

The young woman stood up, undulating, leaving the bed of pillows, from which she watched the sun die behind the autumn trees, and sat down at the piano.

A flight of dead leaves beat against the glass of the huge bay window. The horizon was mourning; bloody clouds ran over the pale sky, setting the twilight on fire like disheveled, defeated flags.

The prelude of *Ysolde* unfolded its rhythms of distraught sobs, of wild unfulfilled rut, of apotheistic death . . . and in the dark room, only illuminated by reflections of the sky in the black water of large mirrors, a delirium of love was unleashed.

In the face of Christiane a mortal rigidity froze the contractions of a supreme anguish, made her a phantom of frenzied pain and passion with the mask of one of Rodin's damned, wearing on the forehead the glittering stigma. And one could have said—with the dangerous status of shapes in the bloody twilight of such an evening—that the harmonic flow came not from the immense black box, like a lordly coffin under its orphrey shrouds strewn with gloomy chrysanthemums . . . but from the slender fingers of the young woman, her complexion that of a sick flower, eyelids liked soiled petals where two crazy eyes blazed, of the whole immobility of her pose and, especially, above all it flowed from her lips, from her lips of wax, from her bloodless, livid lips, from the dull yellow of the dead mucous membranes . . . from her dead lips!

A last moan was choked from the ivory of the keys and the power of the magic potion dissolved into the night.

Then, from the black corner, a man appeared. He was very tall, his gesture exaggerated, pale as the strange musician behind whom he came to kneel. And suddenly, through the whole being of the woman, a shuddering tension electrified her and, arching her loins towards him, she fainted and fell backwards into his vigorous arms, this one word burning her tongue: "Tristan!" Under the enchantment of the musical potion, she was pleased to name him so.

For a long time they looked at each other. A flame was spinning in the eyes of the man, and his bristling, thick red mustache soon devoured her livid lips . . .

For a long while they gazed upon each other. Between them, in the gathering darkness, stretched a line of sulphurous light, from one to the other, as on the first day of their meeting, a year before, and today was their anniversary, this November 2nd, the day of the dead. From one to the other, their souls marched.

A year they had lived alone, in the depths of that deserted countryside, surrounded by a horizon of gloomy forests which, in the summer, was like some sumptuous meadow and, in the winter, like misty, emaciated arms uselessly raised toward the sky. In the large lonely house where they lived in but a few rooms, only the old servants' dull steps dragging in the vast corridors disturbed their funereal tranquility.

A year they had lived alone, far from the accursed crowds, and sumptuously shared their love through their favorite modes of music and poetry. A common horror of Life had bound them together in a mutual dream, the obsession of all their minutes, into this voluntary exile, sheltered from human promiscuities, without the contact of impious hands, without the false sound of living words.

And here they triumphed in the infernal pride of their conquest.

Wallowing in the intoxication of darkness, nerves on fire, they spun in the vertigo of their most intense embraces, as on the edge of insanity's abyss! Possessions never satisfied, of *the Lips alone*, their whole being drunk with incomplete swoons and empty loins, unceasingly terrified by the rebirth of incorruptible desires, slaves to the Law that they themselves dictated to each other: *the Lips alone.*

Their lips! Perpetually fevered kisses altered them, a thirst for blood moistened them with red foam. Their lips! Because of so much biting, so often being pressed together, purple streaks tore them with memories of voracious wounds. Their lips! Through them, they experienced the joy of inexhaustible spasms, the funereal intoxication of the heart which stops beating with too much happiness, the tumultuous pleasure of frustration. And both, their eyes burning with fever, their necks twisting, their hair flaring in the breath of their desires, they appeared like two specters crowned with flowers, cursed by the victory of their dream.

Sometimes, delighted by this delirium, a sensation of non-being chilled them. They sank in cold, deep water, crystal clear, slowly, slowly, to the bed of sand. Then a streamer of seaweed carried them away, chained to each other. Finally, rising to the surface, they floated eternally, lost between life and death, down the river.

Once again their lips pressed against each other with a crackling of sparks, and they sometimes kissed each other like that for whole afternoons, until daybreak. In the shadows then, it was as if a phosphorescent haze emanated from their embrace.

Music frightened them. They rushed madly, in the grooves of forbidden rhythms and perverse harmonies. Sobs choked in their throats at the appearance of patterns laden with memories, and the infernal musician stubbornly pursued them, her murderous fingers making the evocative sounds burst forth, until, exhausted, vibrating all over with the chords, she fell into the expectant arms of the man and bit his lips.

That day, when they unfastened their mouths, a mortal anguish assailed them, an obscure foreboding, a cold terror of something inexorable that awaited them . . . maybe the next revenge of the Norm which they had violated with impunity until then. A flutter of black wings filled the vast room, a storm of greedy beaks banged on the walls.

Shaking, they came to the huge bay window, open onto the twilight. The sunset was like a golden dawn, clouds opened as if by a divine hand, in the bloody mourning of the horizon, and the russet leaves of the high trees seemed redder from this wound of the sky.

Once again, for the last time, they felt confusedly, finally aware of the crime they lived in—they tried to embrace each other, but in vain. A common fall crushed them, shrieking, far from each other, powerless to rejoin. Through supreme desire, they dragged themselves on their knees, their arms outstretched, their lips offered with a rattling cry.

The icy water of the funereal river which they had so often sailed between life and death carried them away. But death now weighed them down, and they were now only two corpses on the sandy bottom, chained by cursed weeds. Eternally thus, they felt themselves turned, not together, stuck to each other's lips as formerly, but each infernally devoured by the same fever of forbidden kisses.

Gripping the thickness of the carpet with her nails, Christiane tried again to reach the man, but a spasm of agony twisted her, and it was he who managed to crawl to her, pressing his lips to his wife's, drinking to the last drop the blood red drool flooding her cheeks . . .

Outside, carried by the night wind, the sounds of a distant bell reached them. The death knell of the office of the dead, this evening of November 2, their anniversary, the day of the dead. It soon became an enormous clamor, shaking the walls, filling their heads with torrential noise. The box of the grand piano vibrated in unison; and the storm of sound carried them away . . . in death . . .

BREAK UP

For A.-M Lauzét.

NOTHING more . . . a sudden appeasement of his whole being after the painful struggle and irremediable words. Nothing more . . . a heavy silence in which a last sob rises from his throat, the definite jolt, as if to vomit his tortured soul. Finally . . . that inert pose of resignation and mourning . . . and I was looking at her, huddled up after her exhausted fall in a corner of the room, pressing her head against the cool walls, like a poor, hurt beast . . .

On the carpet blooms her petal dress, a large dead flower, and she crosses her arms over her chest in a gesture of defending her heart.

Why didn't I come over to look at her? Why didn't I find the strength to utter words of pity? But no, a cold indifference parched me, or perhaps worse, that helplessness which we fall into for having madly excited our nerves with shrill vibrations—to show ourselves as simple and sincere. Ah! The impulses of old, the easy abandonments, the joy of ardent regrets, the infinite voluptuousness of good tears . . . and with the sense of things taking you back, one is then like a man who seeks himself in the night: he feels his shadow, worriedly, in the agonizing expectation of suddenly finding the form of the self as he imagines it, having contemplated himself in the water of mirrors. But the water of mirrors is a liar and he *cannot* recognize himself because he has never *really* seen himself.

Yes! Syllables of tenderness, of pardon, of kindness, tore my throat, rushed to the edge of my lips, but my lips could no longer spell and I fell silent for a long time. I was afraid of the sound of my voice: what intonation could I give it, consistent with my language? Moments flowed, then others, and I continued to look at her, that annihilated form of all my past joys, where it seemed that death had now descended. A soft light played on her pale face, contours lost in the dull cloth of the curtain. Everything was crying in her, her desperate hair crumpled, all the lines composing her appearance collapsed in this funereal inertia. Perhaps I looked at her without seeing her, since this thought crossed my mind: "Is she here, really?" And I did not see her anymore. Deliciously, a vision obsessed me again: Tanagra statuettes in the windows of a collection, visited the day before.

Two young women are near a fountain. One, one knee on the ground, washes and wrings her hair, while the other, standing, spreads on the head of the kneeling one, a small vase of perfumes. A gentle harmony regulates their poses, and under the chaste folds of their dresses one senses happy flesh. Happiness flows in their veins even though they have no hearts. They cherish life without knowing distress, joyful of their pure forms, joyful of the serenity of the sky over their heads, not a vestige of bitterness on their lips . . . This fresh scent in their hair is enough for their coquettish graces and the air is all perfumed from them.

An impression of clear freshness bathed my face: I was living among the serenity of the ancient graces, a pale life, indecisive as the vague polychrome that takes on the frail images, when suddenly the dress of dead flowers blossoming on the floor of the room shivered for a long time. Then a form arose: Lucienne was standing before me. Fever devoured her gaze with a purple shadow, it looked like a veil of mourning thrown on her face, and her cheeks were stained with a blush of delirium. Then all of the nearly one hour past lightly came back to my memory: her smiling arrival at my place, our kisses, our embraces, a foolish dispute over some futile motive, and, with a shrug of my shoulders, the sudden rage of Lucienne, her tears, a fit of sobs, her exhausted fall into the corner of the room from which she had just risen before my eyes in her painful reality.

She looked up at me in despair, and my whole being shuddered with pity. It was, deep inside me, the invasion of a superhuman emotion . . . but it was necessary to make a gesture, to pronounce a word, a single gesture, a single word, and I did not know which ones. Yes, no doubt, take her in my arms, cover her with gentle caresses, drink the fevered tears which trickled from her eyelids. But my arms remained inert. Then, suddenly, in a faltering voice, wet with bitterness, she asked: "Do you have anything to say to me?" And she snuggled against my chest. I squeezed her to suffocate her; anguish strangled my throat, as if something was torn in me, and I panted as if from a painful ascent . . . then there was suddenly the delightful outburst of a melting heart, the whole human being communicating with universal suffering, a shred of the world's soul, and exalted by pity to the intoxication of a god. On the bad soil of a moment ago, on the barren wilderness of my soul, a blossoming of ardent goodness sprang up to the sky. And I kissed Lucienne's hair, I rolled my head against her shoulder, in the hollow of her neck where I had slept so many times, and I grieved for the delirium of that suffering, happy to finally find my heart.

But Lucienne suddenly broke free from my embrace. Impassive, her eyes hard, a mask of contempt and blasphemy on a face that was once drowned in sad sweetness and gloomy happiness, she recoiled slowly, more slowly. The dried tears on her face gave her a calm coolness, and with a gesture of indifference, before the serenity of the mirror, she adjusted her hair. The furrow of unpardonable will was growing on her forehead, and my impulses fell at once.

She left without a word, without a smile, but everything in her said these accursed words: "Our love is dead"; and I watched her go, all graceful and childishly sentimental, amid the rustling of her dress of resurrected flowers.

Alone, an infernal anger shook me, not against her, alas, nor against myself, for both of us were sincere in everything, but against the injustice of life which made us alike, oversensitive souls with identical nerves, passionately doomed to this torture of never suffering the same vibrations except at different times. She and I, bloody food for the pain of everything in the world and in art . . .

THE UNKNOWN YOUNG MAN

For Charles Mourey.

TO Miss Beatrix Burr
The Sunflowers, Putney. London W.

It is from my bed that I write to you, my dear little Miss (knees in the air and very uncomfortable) on the small desk that you were kind enough to send me, and that I use today. The rocking inkwell is a jewel, and the golden leather with peacock feathers which lines the interior enchants me. But where did you find these tones of lacquer, and the *Evening Star* that you painted there? I do not get tired of admiring her. So light, so softly luminous beneath the folds of her floating dress, how well she flies in the twilight sky! And this landscape beneath her, with its pink mountains, peaceful gulfs and a dream city with golden domes! See, I almost wept thinking of you, who are my only tenderness in this world, the only soul who understands me, as I think that you are far from me (for a long time, perhaps forever), when I suffer and am bored.

Yes, far, as far as the beautiful *Star* is, to the people of the enchanted city. However, do not be angry with me, I prefer your absence today because I would never have had the courage to tell you verbally all that I need to tell you. And even then, I feel myself already trembling with the things that I have to tell you, which caused me to stay in bed for two weeks, one of which was spent in a black fever, and nervous fits every half-hour. Just now, before going out, *maman* explicitly forbade me to write. But I think that I would die of my secret if I did not confide it to you immediately.

You would find me changed, little Miss, if you came back. My "wild rose" gaiety, as you called it, went away forever after the crisis that I have just undergone. It is, indeed, a dreadful tragedy which I have witnessed, and of which I seem to have been the cause; that is what despairs me. You, for whom nothing of my heart remains secret, will tell me if I must hold onto this remorse. Yet, be that as it may, I feel that I can no longer be as happy as before, and that the little girl that I had been, that I still was, despite my seventeen years, is no more. All of a sudden, and by the most extraordinary chance, I have been taught the misery of life and pity, and I forever carry in the depths of my heart an indelible memory. Little Miss, do not tell me that these are words and ideas from mere books. I swear to you that I, Georgette, *really feel* this way, not because of the sensibility of some heroine from a novel.

Tomorrow it will be a fortnight since we spent the afternoon at the Rambert's. As always, there were many people there; painters, musicians, numerous English and American women, a lot of young girls looking to marry, all under the patronage of fat Madame Rambert, in her glittering silk dress. Also, as an attraction, the inevitable Duke of Smyrna, presented by Queen Stedman. Naturally, Madame Queen wanted to bring him to me and she was just going to start her usual introduction: "My dear little friend, I introduce to you the Duke of Smyrna . . ." But I immediately turned on my heels, as you know I hate these Tattersall sessions. The fête, however, was charming. A friend of M. Rambert, some sort of explorer-showman, had brought two little exotic dancers who were going to begin soon at Cirque d'Ete. In the garden a Japanese decor had been arranged, with furniture and trinkets from the studio, and they danced on a bamboo platform. It was quite delicious. I was standing aside, in a corner, because of my savageness, and my disgust for female cackling (that I am more and more grateful to you for having impelled in me), and I found myself next to a strange young man. Little Miss, he is the sad character of my drama and I can still remember his alluring features, though to do so makes me weep, as if he were here before me, because he's always been here since, always. And even now I feel that he has loved me more and better than anyone will ever know. I had never seen so much sadness, so much superhuman pain on a living face.

Throughout the afternoon he kept glancing at me, so much so that I was embarrassed by the end—although I did not blame him or think of accusing him of impropriety, on the contrary . . . and I even let myself look at him too, look him in the eyes, as he did me . . . But . . . his eyes, how can I tell you of their desperate flame, their dull madness, their way of resting on mine with such tenderness, imploring a pardon or pity! But what pardon and what pity? And why did I read all this in the eyes of this unknown young man? I asked myself a thousand questions: "Who is he? What is he doing here? Why come out into the world when you have sorrow? And what grief can desolate one so?" . . . etc . . . etc.

Would you believe, for a moment I was going to speak to him out of charity and curiosity, as if, at my first words, he would tell me the cause of his grief and ask me to comfort him, to softly extend my hand. But I felt the impossibility. He, however, continued to look at me, and I thought I saw a tear in his lashes . . . I say "I thought I saw" because was it, possibly, just the effect of this pitying tension the whole of me focused on him? More and more I lost the notion of things.

The dry rhythm of the strange dance, the shine of the clothing and smiles around me, the cheerfulness of the trees and the Japanese decor . . . none of that existed anymore except for the distracted look of this man who reminded me too much of father before he died. That faltering gaze, whose color and movement I had, so to speak, forgotten, was here before my eyes and speaking the mysterious language of an agony. My feelings of these minutes—I cannot manage to specify them to you, now that they are wrapped up in other, darker memories, all bloody, through which I struggle. But I felt an unspeakable disturbance, as if a distant voice called me full of passionate sweetness, murmuring the deepest words . . . And there was no revolt in me, nothing to tear my eyes away from that gaze . . . not modesty, not even a discomfort . . . as the whole world seemed, to me, to have disappeared, vanished, and it seemed to me that we were both alone for eternity, in the void, he and I . . . what am I saying? Not even both of us, but our gazes alone . . .

Finally, we left the Rambert's. *Maman* and I were on the platform of the station of Courcelles, to return to Auteuil. We were pacing while we waited for the train. Always, those two strange eyes were in front of me, fixed on me like a wild hallucination. Over on the other platform, they were there, full of the same desperate flame . . . they embraced me supremely. I wanted to run away from them, but they were obstinate and I could no longer detach my attention. "Am I mad," I asked myself, "or is this a frightening vision?" But no! There he was, really, standing there, leaning his elbow against an iron column, motionless, and still looking at me. And suddenly I saw him coming towards me, slowly crossing the railway . . . but . . . a whistle, the sound of a train chugging, cries of women . . . and he continued to come to me . . . I saw only his eyes, his eyes flooded with tears . . . and then a body that rolls across the rails, beheaded, a burst of bloody scraps that splash my dress . . . and everything is finished . . . I felt myself carried away, half dead . . . the rolling of a wagon . . . heard the tears of *maman* at the foot of my bed . . . For eight days it was thought that I was going mad, with these two words constantly on my lips, that I can still hear myself saying: "The eyes! The eyes!"

Today, I have hardly recovered myself . . . I live in a soft torpor, indifferent to everything, even to that, incapable of realizing exactly what happened. I am afraid, however. Afraid of forgetting. It seems to me, in the confusion I feel, that after such a tragic shake-up of my entire self, it seems to me that nothing has happened, that I have dreamed a bad dream, that's all. And at other times, when the eyes come back, so sweet and so sad, the eyes of the stranger, I start to cry in regret, or perhaps remorse, from a frightful obsession that all the happiness of my life, all my possible happiness, has died with him. And I do not have anyone to talk to about that . . . Ah! My little Miss, console me. Quickly, my little Miss, you who found such good words to dry my tears as a little girl, write to me . . . I cannot tell anything of my sufferings to mom. She would only say that I have lost my head . . . and yet here I am, unhappy, unhappy . . .

I kiss you with all my soul . . . which cries.

Georgette.

THE BOTTLE FROM PAPHOS

For Maurice Barrès.

I spent the morning of January 1st in the archaeological museum of the castle Borely in Marseille, with the little princess Marina.

As I entered the caretaker's house asking to visit (the museum only opened at two o'clock in the afternoon), I found her sitting with familiarity by the fire on a low chair, in a curious dialogue with a fat woman—the guardian's wife, no doubt—and marveling at one of those Provençal crèches with cork houses and polychrome clay figurines of so delicious a naïveté. Quickly, we recognized each other and she reached out to me:

"Are you surprised to find me here? But then, I have changed so much since we last saw each other . . . Will you believe that I adore museums, now that life is no longer enough to excite me . . . but above all the unknown provincial museums where maniacs of art spend their days collecting shards of glory from their little homeland. And, here to Marseille, I came. Shall we go?"

The keeper's wife accompanied us.

Except for some Christian sarcophagi and highly valuable mummy cases, there was little wealth in the museum. But the fine order of the rooms, in this lordly house from the great century, was better than all of the collection. Through the tall, deep windows with small panes, it was a joy to see the blue tablecloth of the Mediterranean crisscross under the yellow winter sun, the hard white outline of the coast, and below us the paths of the French garden, at the foot of the large terrace with baluster, and the immense meadow of the race-course, all deserted without a parade of provincial elegance.

An unleashed mistral swept the blue sky with a rumor, one of those clear storms of the South that beat the walls like battering rams; and in the vast solitary chambers, suffused with mythology, it was like a high whistle accompanying our march.

"Isn't all this deliciously moving, this invisible force?" said the little princess. "As if we are wrapped in terrible kisses . . . and a little deafening, isn't it, like too much blue . . . ?"

She said that, as she said all things, in her too-clear voice that we all knew, reticent with the fear of always revealing too much of herself, despite the beautiful sincerities which she often presented to us. But that morning, I felt her disappointed in her hope of new sensations. Even though she marveled at the battle of lions and centaurs which adorns in bas-relief the tomb dedicated to the memory of Flavius Memorius, comte de Mauritanie, I caught her facetiously moved, lacking exaltation, since in truth the violence of such things frightened her, the harsh harmony of those forms imperfectly suited to that abundant conception which she created for herself and her life. Poor little princess! You would never know how much I pitied you then for your troubles and how much you troubled me there, contemplating your pale, dull rage that was powerless to give birth to the burning moment you sought, the jolt to the nerves you desired so much.

We went through other rooms. Etruscan pottery slept in the showcases, which one passed indifferently, and so dismissed the theory of the Tanagra, which lived its pale, touching and melancholy life there. "What models with veins of divine blood, with the noble impulse of gestures, once posed for these statuettes? And what hands drew them from the nothingness of clay, like an immortal memory of their race, for the charm of our eyes, what artists' hands modeled them, in front of what horizon of pure hills or calm sea, glimpses of forms, readied for the feasts of Madame Venus, in the narrow frame of this little window opening on life?" Ah! Could you not have thought of such marvels, Marina, while we were alone, followed by the dragging footstep of the guardian's old fat woman!

And so already I judged lost, for you and for me, these chosen hours, when we entered a room which occupies the angle of the castle, on the right, on the side looking to the sea. There, really, I suddenly recognized you. A show-case attracted you immediately, irresistibly, and your eyes clung to the vases of pale crystal, all iridescent, streaked with greenish glints and silver reflections, which contained for us the precious drops of the Elixir of Evocation. On a small bottle with a narrow neck, a white label was placed:

Paphos. And your face lit up. The yellow winter sun, then beaming through the glittering murmur of the mistral, struck the frail object. You began to make the gesture of being afraid, as if the terrible force of the wind, carried by the tight ray of the sunbeam, would have threatened the fragile life of the bottle from Paphos. And all of a sudden you became ugly, whose soul was so beautiful, while from your lips fell the enchantment of those immortal verses of the poet Stéphane Mallarmé:

> *My old tome closed upon the name Paphos,*
> *I take delight in summoning by pure genius*
> *a ruin blessed with myriad ocean sprays*
> *beneath the distant hyacinth of its triumphal days.*

Outside, the wind was raging and I watched the sea, foaming against the white islands of the gulf. You remained motionless, too thrilled in your whole being, so that no words other than those divine, like that which formerly agitated your lips, might come from you. And you, a fragile creature before the fragile eternity of the bottle from Paphos, there on that first painful day of a new year, the day when so much melancholy penetrates the soul and keeps it bitter for months, probably thought:

"Are the perfumes this crystal contained that powerful to move me so, after so many centuries? And me, the dreams and the emotions that agitated me, and all that I was, and all that I am, and all that I will be, until the time when death will break me, of all that—nothing will survive then, and so many beautiful impulses will remain vain!"

But a voice told you, a maternal voice, the good counselor of every minute when we are afraid of death . . . that voice said:

"Nothing dies in bodies that reflected ardent souls, any more than crystal vases in which strong perfumes were enclosed. They shatter those that never contained the almighty elixir. If you can contemplate intact this bottle of Paphos, it is because tears were poured inside it, the tears of some great love or thought . . ."

And I saw the princess Marina draw from her sleeve a fine handkerchief of cambric to wipe her beautiful, wounded eyes . . .

THE CONVICT

For Mrs. Jeanne Jacquemin.

A long troop of convicts paraded on the towpath where I came each morning, in crystalline light, to stroll through my memory and rest my weary spirit among the dead thistles and dry grass, miserable vegetation that mirrored my heart. A common rope tied them by the hands, one behind the other, a single chain of hemp rotted by the humidity of the prison.

They passed singing. Where did they come from and where were they going? From which prison to what place of dark torture . . . or perhaps back to the train station that has momentarily freed them, its roof shining in the trees there . . .

There must have been two, three . . . perhaps even four hundred. Their mournful chain passed interminably on the bank, all similar forms lacking color and moving with an even gait, their clothes dusty, wearing the haughty faces of resignation, docile weakness, and lamentable sweetness that follow a life of failed revolt.

They moved to the rhythm of their plaintive song. It spoke of birds and flowers, pure caresses and confessions, clouds and regrets . . . and on the pale lips of these men it blossomed like a bouquet by the shimmering river, in the glow of the pale meadows, floating over the happy peace of the little village nearby.

In a narrow window a young girl appeared, attracted by the song. But soon her face turned pale to see what mouths uttered it, and hers was the only human pity displayed for the passing accursed.

Plunged in the depths of their misery, they did not see her as she stripped the flowers in her window-box with her charming hands, blessing them.

Only, one of them *did* see her, the last of them all, he who passed close to me. He alone was different than the others. Of small size, strangely blond (almost white-haired, which gave him the appearance of a precocious old man) with a flame of hatred burning in his gaze. His eyes defined him entirely, so much so that he appeared to be a man living outside this world, in the delirium of a powerful dream.

He seemed to see nothing, to look at nothing at all, not the landscape surrounding him, the soft splendor of the sky over his head, his companions of infamy, not even his chain. The river flowed, slow, limpid and without a ripple, as he gazed at her in ecstasy, his soul and eyes drunk on her magic reflection, the only true reality capable of casting a charm over man. An infinity of sky, the abyss spotted with a calm flight of far off clouds, was irresistibly attractive. He seemed dizzied by this clear vision, so compelling in its crystalline sharpness: the frail reeds barely curved in the slight current, the thatch of a washhouse, a waiting rowboat and the sharp angle of an oar reflected, small still houses, and the window . . . the open window through which the girl was bending . . . and the shower of flowers which, as they fell in the reflection, seemed to rise into the blue chasm of the sky! What painful memories of the man's abandoned heart, or a late blooming of hope, floated up with them?

When he raised his eyes, I saw they were drowned in a flood of tears, as if he was pouring out the suffering of his whole life, and this supreme joy had transfigured him, enlightening his being and enabling him to cry again, to find his heart after so many years of death! In the depths of his eyes, that flame of hate had been extinguished.

Then I raised myself to study him. Standing on the bank and treading on the dry grass, the white gold of his hair burning in the light, he stood clothed with holy grandeur, resplendent with superhuman beauty. As the sunlight played across the dust of his ignominious uniform, precious pearls glowed, and this man marked with an accursed seal might have been taken, from afar, for some strange god in a tattered tunic.

The others continued in their mechanical walk, foreheads lowered, inattentive to the world. But the blond convict stopped. For a moment, our eyes met and he stared at me obstinately, contempt on his lips, and suddenly the flame of hate flared in his face again. Shudders of revulsion shook him and, with a jerk of his arms in a sudden gesture, he snapped the hempen rope, dropping among the tall grasses to hide near me.

However, the troops continued to march and no one had seen the escape. From the edge of the ground where he had dropped, the blond convict scarcely raised his head, heavy with despair and anxiety, and plunged it under the dead tufts until, torn by thistles, he finally raised it triumphantly in the sunlight.

On the other shore, the window had just closed. A painful sob stifled in the man's throat, and then he took my hands and these febrile words came from him: "Are you afraid . . . of me? No, do not be afraid. They are already gone and I am saved. Here I am, free! Finally free. Ah, I do not flee anymore, it is all these reflections that have made me crazy! These reflections, this calm light, the charm of this landscape and she, just now, at this window, tearing those petals for me! For me!"

And he continued, his hair wild and disheveled: "To be free! Do you know why I wanted this freedom? To avenge myself on life! Listen to me: I was young, I suffered, I loved. I had the rage to suffer, the rage to love, a need to blindly give myself to others, a madness to be good. I was good! And then, oh! I do not remember what happened, but I remember that there was a woman in my story . . . yes, yes, yes! She was too beautiful.

"Then, one evening, out of hatred for her beauty which martyred me, one evening—there was red moonlight in a snowy sky—I killed her. What a joy to see her disfigured, twisted by the long agony that I desired, and then what paradise as her two eyes sprung open, and a line of blood clotted around her neck . . .

"I had never loved her so much. But everyone forgets, and for twenty years I had forgotten her. Otherwise I would have wanted my freedom too soon. But twenty years ago I did not have tears . . . and did not know how to remember . . . without crying . . ."

In the distance of the plain, at the end of the great pale meadows, the gray line of men was still passing, and soon disappeared behind a tuft of trees.

He went on, very calmly: "I must tell you that we go out alone, often without guards. The common chain is sufficient, and no one dares to escape, for it is a law we all follow that if one of us breaks it, the others must stone him.

"Fortunately, they were still drunk this morning, as yesterday we celebrated the warden's feast. Now, here I am, free!"

Happily, he raised both his hands towards the sky, an ecstasy of apotheosis delighting him. And he cried: "Yes, I'll be able to kill again, to kill Beauty! No longer to avenge myself—for I was mad in telling you that just now, lying to myself in idiotic vanity—but out of *pleasure*! Yes, for pleasure!"

Then he left. For a long time I watched him, until he was nothing but a black dot on the horizon, like a cursed flower in an immense lake of pale meadows.

AUTUMN BEACH

For Abel Hermant.

ROSE-MARY TO LUCIENNE

EIGHT days already, oblivious and forgetful woman, without news of you! Where are you? Still walking your cottage snobbery through cosmopolitan casinos . . . instead of joining me, as you had so heartily promised. Too bad for you. Anyway, this is the last of my reproaches: firstly, because I already saw you adopt that drifting look, and then also because all of this is the worst form of epistolary literature. We are too much like those who spend their chronicles telling you that they lack a subject, exhaust their one hundred and fifty lines in utter distress, and end up by exclaiming: "Here I see that my column is accomplished! . . ."

So, quickly, about us; otherwise all the pretty things that I have to say to you will be gone . . . and then you can go and chase after them! Why do you smile skeptically? They are the only things in life that are amusing, these ephemeral nothings: the bits of landscape and passion, the glimpses of sky and flesh, the infinitesimal of everything, the insignificances, all of that has almost no reason to be. Have you not felt many times that our entire happiness or sadness can come in the rustling of a blade of grass, in the passage of a cloud, in the caprice of an open or closed door?

I regret you are not here. The beach is deserted; there is no one left (there has never been anyone, for that matter), no one at all. That is to say, I exaggerate, for, including me, we are just twelve or fifteen lingering here. If you could see the desolate look of the cabins on the sand. They are bored, set far at a respectful distance from each other, like people who have not been introduced, their cyclopean faces turned towards the eternal Ocean. It's gray days here, with the sneaking sun heating up the heavy clouds. How to use the time? No casino, no friends; the natives are true savages, fortunately! They live apart, each in a home behind closed doors, far from each other, like the cabins on the beach. Finally, I find myself alone, all alone, and that enchants me. I get up early; I go on long walks; I discover unknown corners (look, the other day, I found a marvel: a small valley inaccessible in the hollow of a cliff, and just as big as your hand, all blooming with crazy flowers, brought there by the wise wind from the coast). And I read, I read to become a fool. I read everything, right and wrong, pure psychologists and mixed psychologists, symbolists and naturalists, the sumptuous and the simplistic, mystics and sensationalists, and I love them all equally. This is all that remains: we forget ourselves better when we lose ourselves in the dreams of others.

My cabin is the last one, on the right when you look at the sea, at the foot of a huge black rock which, in the morning, protects me with its ghastly shadow. I filled it with English cretonne (the jewel of cretonne), purple poppies in a haze of withered herbs. I spend all my time there, among this light decoration which corresponds so wholly to my momentary "moods." That's where I write you from. My door is wide open to the sea; the water is a moiré of green and pearl-gray, the color of my dress last winter, remember? The sky is blue behind a mist of milk, the blue of the month of May under white gauze. And you cannot imagine the beautiful, profound complaint in the disturbing love-melody of the waves. So many discreet tears, regrets, confessions, dear and grand words are murmuring, grieving, in it, and all the dizzying sweetness of eternal oaths that life carries, and all the distress of nostalgia! Ah, that good voice, indulgent and maternal; she consoles and encourages, she cradles and caresses. To listen to her thus, at length, I feel invaded by delicious emotions. A feeling of pity for everyone and everything softens me; all the pettiness of a woman, *our* pettiness of rancor or enthusiasm, our weaknesses, our foolishness, all that we are, ridiculous and incomplete, all this fades into me. I believe myself once again the naïve and indecisive little girl of old, a primitive creature capable of all sincerities, of all impulses, with, additionally, an abundant understanding of life in its beauty and grandeur. The wind has just closed my door: here I am still more alone, in my little house of planks. Languor wins me, a divine lassitude . . . the pen trembles at the end of my fingers . . . crack . . . this big ink scarab . . . I am almost asleep . . .

Suddenly, close to me, outside, probably on the beach or on some bark, there is a voice singing . . . accompanied by a harmonium. She sings I do not know what, I do not know anymore . . . (maybe I am dreaming). *It will return, the time of cherries*, and I listen, surprised, terrified. A silence. The voice resumes: *I'm a colonel's widow* . . . and the harmonium pushes its muffled squeals, incomplete chords that run out of steam, dominated by the sound of the waves. I open the door of my cabin: opposite, on the sand, a woman is sitting in front of the instrument, while another, standing, sings. They are ugly, dressed in black, wearing the hats of the Salvationists. As soon as she perceives me, the one who sings leaves her place, approaches, while continuing to push her thin notes, and then remains motionless. It's over: the harmonium sobs a last chuckle, a snarling, stubborn note, and then hisses. The musician gets up too; they are both looking at me, mute, without a gesture. I give them a white coin: they bow, bow like automatons, then each seizes one side of the instrument of torture and they go before another cabin to restart their personal trade. Unfortunately, the house is empty; both, this time, shout in an inspired duet: but in vain. And they leave, with new hope.

I told you that my beach is a beach of surprises.

I left the day before yesterday, very early. These autumn mornings have an adorable freshness. Mists float in trees that have barely been cleared; in the distance, on the side of the wood, there are already spots of rust which indicate the sap is dying. The sea itself seems withered, dull green, livid, striped with gray. After two hours of walking, I arrive at a miniature village, deserted. Nobody is in the only street I cross. The closed windows are sad, with funereal airs. Everyone is in the fields or out at sea. I wander for some time in this solitude and suddenly I am in a large pen where sawyers are working. It's the only sound of life, the regular sound of saws in the wood. There are about ten of them: they look very small; they look like articulated puppets. Their rhythmic movement seems to be regulated by one of those sand-mill wheels that start children's cardboard constructions. And suddenly they all sing in unison. A song rises, a popular song, with limpid charm like this sky, now stripped of its cover of fog. A song which has remained in my spirit, though I only heard them sing it once, so full of naïve sadness and simple melancholy. Between each verse, only the sound of the saws persists; then the air resumes, sluggish and dreary like a tired complaint. Oh, those monotonous notes, the resumption of the refrain which strips each stanza of its indifferent gaiety . . . they remain in my memory, unforgettable. I'll sing their song to you, and you'll see . . .

> *There's nothing as friendly*
> *Lan faï lan cru lan farira,*
> *There's nothing as friendly*
> *As a cute pit sawyer,*
> *Lan faï lan cru lan farira,*
> *As a cute pit sawyer.*
>
> *The master comes to see*
> *Lan faï lan cru lan farira,*
> *The master comes to see*
> *Courage, my companions,*
> *Lan faï lan cru lan farira,*
> *Courage, my companions.*

My wife is unfaithful,
Lan faï lan cru lan farira,
My wife is unfaithful,
I push her in the sea
Lan faï lan cru lan farira,
I push her in the sea

Sing, all you sirens, sing,
Lan faï lan cru lan farira,
Sing, all you sirens, sing:
You are so right to sing,
Lan faï lan cru lan farira,
You are so right to sing.

You have the sea to drink,
Lan faï lan cru lan farira,
You have the sea to drink
And my wife to consume,
Lan faï lan cru lan farira,
And my wife to consume.

But the poetry of that, in the open air, sung by those ten voices of men who toil in this enclosure of dry grass, blue thistles and faded suns, by the nostalgic light of this autumn morning, how do I express it to you in words? And I came back home sadly, and for two days kept a delicious bitterness in my whole being . . . so much that in writing to you of it, I am once again foundering . . .

So, embracing the feeling, I hasten to put my final point down here: see you soon.

REVENGE OF THE LIGHT

For Gustave Guiches.

FROM birth I was doomed to the slavery of Darkness.

I came into the world on a stormy summer night, the darkest night which had ever fallen on the earth in human memory. Not the beneficent glow of a star pierced the funereal pall of the firmament. A thick, heavily sticky atmosphere stifled men, and in the nearby countryside herds died of terror. Nature had gone into mourning to welcome my coming.

My childhood was spent in the shadow of a big closed house, in the middle of an ancient park that enveloped it in darkness. An incurable eye disease afflicted my mother. For years she had lived in two rooms on the second floor, where a perpetual night reigned, barely lit by the indistinct radiance of night lights veiled with green silk. It was there that I spent my days, in that gloom in which the faces of the few animated beings took on, in the play of green reflections, the livid hardness of a corpse. My mother's hair was all white, although she was still young. I can still see her, as she appeared to me every day for ten years, dressed in loose light dresses, coming and going on the silent carpets and almost always sitting or, rather, half-extended, on an Empire-styled couch in the shape of a sleigh with a goose neck. My happiness was to squat in front of her, for hours, to feel the caresses of her hand in my hair. Serious thoughts, deep and sweet, fell from her pale lips, which my childish unconsciousness collected and which, remembered, remain to me the surest refuge against the cruelties or contempt of others. She often spoke to me of my father, who had died just two months before my birth. She evoked him as of an anemic race, very tall and pale, carrying in his veins a blood of neurosis, of a nostalgic and painful heredity. She showed me a portrait of him, a daguerreotype with metallic reflections, where he returned to life, seated in a pensive pose, holding an open book in his hand. Tears flooded my mother's face. I raised myself to her cheeks to kiss her, as though intoxicated. Ah! It is from having drank too much from these tears that the strange thirst for the tears of others has come to me, and that fanatical pity, which has no repugnance, for all suffering beings I see. We remained thus for a long time, confounded and sobbing with the same sobs. Sometimes a delirium shook the delicate woman and she took my head in her soft hands, looking at me and repeating, "You will look like him . . . yes!" And she covered me with caresses. In fact, gradually, it seemed to me, that the resemblance was born in me: had I not drunk, maternal despair reverberating through such precious tears, the very image of my dead father?

However, we continued to live in the shadow of the big, closed house. When I was led outside, I was seized with the nervous shocks that the full clarity of sight gave me, and each time it took eight days to recover from my delirious fever. For my puerile caprices, for my foolishness, the only punishment for a long time was the threat of light, so the memory of my first sunlit landscape persists in me like a terror. I was eight years old. One burning August day, when the light was of blinding intensity, we had closed the shutters of the whole house against it, and let down the curtains in front of the windows. As the heat exasperated my nerves, I stumbled into a dry stubbornness with I do not know what motive. Neither the prayers nor the threats of my mother could quench it, so then, desperate, she sent for the gardener and ordered him to take me by force in his arms and to carry me away, my head covered with a shawl, into the full sunlight, there to abandon me. In vain I tried to struggle, fruitlessly I snuggled against the chaise longue where the dear woman rested (it did not seem possible to me that this refuge could be violated), then into the space near her bed, and then in the deepest, shadowy corner of the room. All in vain. My mother was inexorable and, even today, after so many years, in reliving this memory I cannot help but blame her, to reproach her for that cruelty.

So the gardener took me away. I revolted, screamed, cried, begged, all to soften him, but he held me tightly. I took revenge on him by kicking him in the belly and landing blows on the back of his neck. A few minutes elapsed and I felt myself being laid down on a bench, someone removing the cloth that covered my head, and screaming as I closed my eyes with my hands. How long did I remain like that? I do not remember. I felt the sensation, despite the heat of the air, of having been suddenly plunged into a bath of icy water. I shivered, my teeth chattered, I felt a stinging, agonizing pain in the depths of my head. Even though I closed my eyes, sank my fists into them, one image tormented me; scarcely seen, but persistent and cruel, and I found myself alone on a terrace, on a level with the park, enclosed by a low wall covered with ivy and decorated with vases of marble. Beyond, the immense plain opened, a rolling sea of oily vegetation under a powdery whirlwind of clarity. Hills closed off the horizon with soft lines that seemed to waver in the light. And everything was moving around me. I tried a few steps but vertigo made me stagger. I was caught in a whirlwind of burning and implacable life that rolled me, rolled me, carrying me away. And despite the wound that I felt in my eyes, so sharp and so vivid that I wiped my face as if it had been flooded with blood and, indeed, dazzled, I saw my hands red and quivering; despite the torture that the vision of this rain of sun was inflicting on my whole being, I could not help but keep my eyes wide open, to become intoxicated by the marvelous spectacle. I found myself alone for the first time in my life. Pride swelled in my chest for I was not afraid, for I dared come face to face with the terrible enemy whose vengeance I had unconsciously feared, and which had filled my childhood with so much terror and worry: the Light. Bravely, I advanced towards the parapet of ivy: the terrace projected over the plain for ten or twelve meters. Powerful winds came to me, filled my mouth, caressed my skin, like a breeze from the open sea, which brings scents of countries unknown. The meadows rustled under the wind's passage and it seemed as if a life animated them, making them bend and recover in significant gestures. The memory of the great rooms drowned in shadows where I had lived until then, the dark house and the ghostly beings, faded in me, and I thought of my mother only to wish her there, near me, to share the delicious and whirling drunkenness.

With what sweet kindness, with what anxious tenderness the Light cradled and caressed me! It entered me as one drinks a cordial, and I ran my tongue on my lips to savor it better, to better know the taste, so that it would remain unforgettable. Had I never before felt alive? Did I only now realize that I was a human being, different from others, capable of thinking and feeling thrilled myself? From the hollows of maternal dresses had exalted an ignorant sensibility which found no place to learn from but in the depressive sadness of a sick woman. The glimmering glow of the green night lights that lit up her mute life were no longer the only light that lit the world!

Now a balm seeped into my eyelids, flowed to heal the wound of my eyes, and it was like a sweet music of joy singing in my head, inside me, or outside of me? This is how the Light, a generous and redeeming vengeance that slung me from the slavery of the shadow in which faded the fragile flower of my life, made me the equal of the other beings of the earth who I thought, naïvely, admired and adored the light, like me. Alas, I learned later, and at what price, the truth to be the opposite!

Little by little, however, the day was falling. Behind me, great stretches of shadow were spread over the trees of the park, and the slow march of night conquered the plain. All luminous joy would soon expire in a sob, quickly stifled by twilight. In spite of myself, I remained still, leaning on the ivy terrace from which I had just learned of the living splendor of the sky. It was of a veiled serenity, a chaste and simple color, like the dresses of my mother, where I had loved so much to take refuge. But suddenly a wound opened, flaming with blood, which quickly spread all over the horizon, and the sun was dying. The devouring darkness ran under the once glittering vault, and the night overflowed. Then I was afraid of the shadows, as I had been afraid of the light, and closed my eyes, to see again the liberating radiance of the sun, which now lived in me . . .

A PARTIAL LIST OF SNUGGLY BOOKS

G. ALBERT AURIER *Elsewhere and Other Stories*
CHARLES BARBARA *My Lunatic Asylum*
S. HENRY BERTHOUD *Misanthropic Tales*
LÉON BLOY *The Desperate Man*
LÉON BLOY *The Tarantulas' Parlor and Other Unkind Tales*
ÉLÉMIR BOURGES *The Twilight of the Gods*
CYRIEL BUYSSE *The Aunts*
JAMES CHAMPAGNE *Harlem Smoke*
FÉLICIEN CHAMPSAUR *The Latin Orgy*
FÉLICIEN CHAMPSAUR
    The Emerald Princess and Other Decadent Fantasies
BRENDAN CONNELL *Unofficial History of Pi Wei*
BRENDAN CONNELL *The Metapheromenoi*
RAFAELA CONTRERAS *The Turquoise Ring and Other Stories*
ADOLFO COUVE *When I Think of My Missing Head*
QUENTIN S. CRISP *Aiaigasa*
LADY DILKE *The Outcast Spirit and Other Stories*
CATHERINE DOUSTEYSSIER-KHOZE *The Beauty of the Death Cap*
ÉDOUARD DUJARDIN *Hauntings*
BERIT ELLINGSEN *Now We Can See the Moon*
ERCKMANN-CHATRIAN *A Malediction*
ALPHONSE ESQUIROS *The Enchanted Castle*
ENRIQUE GÓMEZ CARRILLO *Sentimental Stories*
EDMOND AND JULES DE GONCOURT *Manette Salomon*
REMY DE GOURMONT *From a Faraway Land*
REMY DE GOURMONT *Morose Vignettes*
GUIDO GOZZANO *Alcina and Other Stories*
GUSTAVE GUICHES *The Modesty of Sodom*
EDWARD HERON-ALLEN *The Complete Shorter Fiction*
EDWARD HERON-ALLEN *Three Ghost-Written Novels*
RHYS HUGHES *Cloud Farming in Wales*
J.-K. HUYSMANS *The Crowds of Lourdes*
J.-K. HUYSMANS *Knapsacks*
COLIN INSOLE *Valerie and Other Stories*
JUSTIN ISIS *Pleasant Tales II*